Quintin Craufurd

Sketches chiefly relating to the history, religion, learning, and manners of the Hindoos

With a concise account of the present state of the native powers of Hindostan. Vol. 1

Quintin Craufurd

Sketches chiefly relating to the history, religion, learning, and manners of the Hindoos
With a concise account of the present state of the native powers of Hindostan. Vol. 1

ISBN/EAN: 9783337264017

Printed in Europe, USA, Canada, Australia, Japan

Cover: Foto ©Andreas Hilbeck / pixelio.de

More available books at **www.hansebooks.com**

SKETCHES

CHIEFLY RELATING TO THE

HISTORY, RELIGION, LEARNING, AND MANNERS,

OF THE

HINDOOS.

WITH

A concise Account of the PRESENT STATE of the NATIVE POWERS of HINDOSTAN.

THE SECOND EDITION, ENLARGED.

IN TWO VOLUMES.

VOL. I.

LONDON:

PRINTED FOR T. CADELL, IN THE STRAND.

MDCCXCII.

ADVERTISEMENT.

IT is not my intention in the following
sheets, to add to the number of authors
who have devoted their labours to the history of the conquerors of Hindostan ; but
to draw the attention of the Public, for a
moment, from the exploits of Mahomedans
and Europeans, and direct it to the original inhabitants of that country. If this
attempt should lead to further inquiry upon
so interesting a subject, or be productive of
any pleasure or information to the Reader,
I shall think my pains well bestowed, as my
wishes will be accomplished.

THE AUTHOR.

N. B. *In reading the names of persons and
places, the vowels are understood to be
pronounced as in Italian.*

B 2

☞ *The* Vignette *in the* Title-page *is a View in the* subterraneous Temple *in the* Island *of* Elephanta.

☞ *The* Vignette *in the* Title-page *is a View in the* subterraneous Temple *in the* Island *of* Elephanta.

ADVERTISEMENT

TO THIS

SECOND EDITION.

SINCE the First Edition of this Work was published, I have read in the Second Volume of the Transactions of the Royal Society at Edinburgh, *Remarks on the Astronomy of the Brahmans, by Mr. Playfair*; and in the First Volume of the Asiatic Researches, *Remarks on the Gods of Greece, Italy, and India, by Sir William Jones.* I regret that I had not seen these works in time to have made that use of them in the First Edition, which I have taken the liberty of doing in this.

From the materials furnished by Monsieur le Gentil and Monsieur Bailly, Mr. Playfair has even gone beyond those authors, in establishing, by scientific proof, the originality

ginality

ginality of the Hindoo aftronomy, and its fuperior antiquity to any other that is known; while Sir William Jones has made great progrefs to fhew, that the mythology of the Egyptians, Greeks, and Romans, derived its origin from the fertile imaginations of the Hindoos.

The Edition I now offer to the Public was already prepared for the prefs, and given into the hands of a friend to read, when I was informed, that an Hiftorical Difquifition concerning India, by Dr. Robertfon, would foon be publifhed. The name of a man fo eminent in the literary world, naturally made me anxious to fee this work, and eafily induced me to fufpend the publication of my own. It is needlefs to fay how much I was flattered by the notice Dr. Robertfon has taken of the SKETCHES CONCERNING HINDOSTAN. But, after due confideration, I thought it beft to fuffer this Edition to go to the prefs *exactly*

fuch

ſuch as it was previous to my peruſal of the Diſquiſition of the elegant Hiſtorian, and to reſerve to myſelf the liberty of making ſuch remarks upon it in the Notes, as might appear neceſſary.

An apology is certainly due from me to the Purchaſers of the Firſt Edition, for not having the new matter, that is introduced into the Second, printed ſeparately, for their accommodation : and I cannot help expreſſing my regret that this was rendered impoſſible, by the neceſſity of intermixing the greateſt part of it with what was already publiſhed.

The moſt conſiderable Additions have been made in the Firſt Sketch, on the Hiſtory and Religion of Mankind ; in the Seventh, on the Mythology; and in the Eleventh, on the Aſtronomy of the Brahmans. The Thirteenth and Fourteenth Sketches are entirely new. For the account of the Man-

ners

ners and Religion of Thibet, which appears in the Thirteenth Sketch, I am indebted to the kindnefs of Robert Bogle Efquire, who, in the politeft manner, permitted me to make what ufe I pleafed of the interefting manufcripts of his brother, the late Mr. James Bogle. I thought it, however, my duty to reftrain my inclination to communicate the whole to the Public, and have inferted only fuch extracts as tended to elucidate the immediate object of my enquiry.

Q. CRAUFURD.

London,
June 12, 1791.

CONTENTS

OF THE

FIRST VOLUME.

Vol. I. a

SKETCH

S K E T C H I.

---

*General Reflections on the History and
Religion of Mankind.*

THERE is perhaps no subject which
has given rise to more speculative
inquiry, than the formation of the earth,
and the origin of the human race: still the
most ingenious systems are, in reality, but
philosophical romances; they have never risen
above probable conjecture, unsubstantiated
by proof. In few instances we can trace
the period when even those nations were
formed, who, in their progress or their

VOL. I.   B   decline,

decline, have filled an important place in history; while the origin of the greatest part of the inhabitants of the earth is entirely hid in obscurity. Inquiry has in vain attempted to ascertain from whence the innumerable tribes and powerful nations came, that were found established in the western hemisphere; to find out who gave inhabitants to the many detached islands discovered in ancient and modern times; and to account for the difference of features, of complexion, and of hair, existing between the European, the Hindoo, the Caffer, and the American.

We are told that Manco Capac civilized a tribe of wild Peruvians, which afterwards became a numerous and happy nation; that this nation was subdued, its princes and nobles destroyed, its people massacred, with the ferocity of beasts of prey, by men who professed a religion, the chief charac-
teristic

teriftic of whofe doctrines is meeknefs and humanity *.

Perhaps the origin of all nations, though their fubfequent hiftory may be different, is fimilar to that of the Peruvians. A number of perfons, by accident or compact, affociate and form a tribe; others unite with it, or are compelled to fubmit to its increafing power: but how the individuals came into the country, is generally a problem which cannot be folved; and though philofophy may attempt to explain, and in the fruitfulnefs of imagination may find connexions and refemblances, after the moft laborious refearch, we muft ftop, and reft fatisfied with this truth, That the Supreme Being, who created the univerfe, peopled *our* planet in a manner conformable to his

---

* The enormities which were then committed, cannot be attributed to the character of the nation, but to the reigning fanaticifm of the time, and the avarice of particular leaders.

B 2 wifdom,

wifdom, though hid from its fhort-fighted inhabitants.

In endeavouring to trace the rife and progrefs of religion and laws, of arts and fciences, we are likewife frequently ftopped in our inquiries, or led into error, by the gloom that in general hides their firft origin.   We may fometimes imagine that we have difcovered analogies, and may argue in confequence of them, when perhaps no other analogy exifts, than that which arifes, from thofe innate faculties and principles which nature has implanted in the mind of man, and are common to every people and climate.

There is no nation, I believe, however barbarous it may be*, nor any individual, whatever for the fake of falfe celebrity he

may

---

* Though fome writers have mentioned nations fo barbarous, as to have no idea of a Supreme Being, or of a future exiftence, yet I am inclined to believe that

this

may pretend, who has not a fenfe, infe-
parable from his exiftence, of a fupreme
ruling power; and this internal evidence
of the dependence of the human race upon
a fuperior Being, is a natural and fufficient
bafis to fupport a fyftem of religious worfhip.

------

this opinion has arifen from a want of fufficient acquaintance with the nations they fpeak of; as I have
myfelf known many inftances, in which an opinion,
haftily received, has, upon nearer connexion, been found
to be erroneous.   An eminent Author, Dr. Robertfon,
has faid, that tribes have been difcovered in America
who have no idea of a Supreme Being, and no rites of
religious worfhip; but he has afterwards alfo faid, that
" the idea of the immortality of the foul can be traced
" from one extremity of America to the other, and
" that the moft uncivilized of its favage tribes do not
" apprehend death to be the extinction of being."
Garcilaffo de la Vega, who was born at Cuzco fhortly
after its conqueft, who was of the family of the Incas,
but brought up a Chriftian, fays, that the Peruvians believed in the exiftence of a Supreme Being, and in a
ftate of rewards and punifhments. The fame is afferted by many authors with refpect to the Mexicans.

B 3   The

The neceſſity of eſtabliſhed rules for the government of every ſociety or claſs of people, is ſo evident, that the rudeſt tribes muſt have ſoon perceived, that they neither could enjoy internal peace and ſafety without them, nor be in a ſtate to defend themſelves againſt attacks from abroad: and hence the origin of laws and government.

When tribes or ſocieties are formed, and their immediate wants ſupplied, as men live and communicate with each other, the mode of providing for them is improved; leſs urgent and nicer wants ſucceed; thought is exerted; the faculties of the mind unfold, by being employed; talents are awakened, by being called for and encouraged; and nations, from their real and imaginary wants, and exertions to ſupply them, gradually go on to luxury and to refinement. When the inventions that took their riſe from neceſſity and convenience,

nience, have been carried fo far, as to leave genius at leifure to gratify itfelf with fubjects of curiofity and amufement, it takes a more exalted courfe; the liberal arts follow, and proceed on towards perfection; until fome of thofe revolutions to which nations are fubject, arreft their progrefs, and again bury them in oblivion. Such was their fate in Egypt, in Greece, and in Italy.

All the religions we are acquainted with, lay claim to a divine origin: all that are found eftablifhed in civilized nations, ordain the adoration of God, and, with little other variation, than fuch as may depend on climate or local circumftances, inculcate fuch duties of morality, as tend to preferve order in fociety, and procure happinefs to the individual. It might be expected, that an inftitution in its nature fo facred, and fo evidently neceffary to the peace and welfare of mankind,. would be lefs liable than any

B 4

other

other to perverfion or abufe : but though nothing can more ftrongly evince the dominion of our paffions over our reafon, we every where find that religion has, more or lefs, been made fubfervient to their gratification, and employed to impofe on the credulous multitude. If we fee the Brahman in Hindoftan ufing the fuperftition he has created, to procure to himfelf and his order certain diftinctions and privileges, we have feen the Chriftian prieft doing the fame: and, however melancholy the reflection may be, the decline of refpect for that religion, which in itfelf is fo pure, may principally be afcribed to the pride and mifconduct of its minifters.

The profeffors of the Chriftian, the Mahomedan, and the Hindoo religion *, form

by

---

* There are many reafons which lead us to fuppofe, that the inhabitants of Pegu, Siam, Thibet, and even China

by far the greateſt portion of the inhabitants of the globe. In compariſon with the number of the followers of any of theſe, every other religious denomination, as far as has been hitherto aſcertained, may be looked upon as inconſiderable. Hiſtory has recorded the origin, and marked the progreſs, of the two former; but the riſe of the latter, and the changes it may have undergone, are placed at a period ſo remote, and we are yet ſo defective in materials, that it is impoſſible to follow its ſteps with the ſame preciſion, that may be expected in treating of the others.

The effects of the doctrines of the Khoran are too well known to require a parti-

____

China and Japan, derived their religion from the ſame ſource with the Hindoos. The analogy between the worſhip of the people of Pegu and Siam, and that of the Hindoos, is ſo palpably evident, as not to leave any doubt of their common origin. See SKETCH XIII, &c.

cular

cular difcuffion. They were delivered to an unenlightened people, by a daring and artful man, who profanely affected to have an intercourfe with the Deity, and to be particularly felected by him to convey his will to mankind. He fupported this fabulous revelation with pretended vifions and miracles, which, though defpifed by us for their groffnefs and abfurdity, operated with great effect on the more ignorant Arabians. He commanded belief, punifhed difobedience, and every faithful Muffulman thought it a pious duty to fubdue thofe by the fword, who refufed to embrace his religion. The leaders of the early Mahomedans, being active and intrepid warriors, at the head of a hardy race of men, whom they had infpired with fanatic courage, like a torrent bore down all who attempted to oppofe them, and in an aftonifhingly fhort fpace of time carried their dominion and their faith into every quarter of the then known world.

Science,

Science, as far as the Mahomedan religion spread, felt its baneful influence; and still wherever we find the banner of the crescent raifed, we fee it followed by an enflaved, ignorant, and bigotted race of men, whofe hiftory, excepting where it is faintly enlightened by a few Arabian writers, creeps through one continued gloom of cherifhed barbarifm.

At a time when the Roman empire was at the fummit of its power, when learning and the arts were admired and encouraged, and the worfhip of the gods in its utmoft fplendor, the Chriftian religion was ufhered into the world in a remote and inconfiderable province, under the mildeft and moft humble afpect.

Thofe who were chofen to promulgate it to mankind, were taken from the loweft claffes of a people, who had fcarcely excited the attention of their more polifhed conquerors, by any thing but their turbulence and

and obstinacy. The Apostles, now so justly
held in high veneration by us, then unknown and undistinguished, except within
the humble sphere of their Christian con-
verts, were, with their opinions, little noticed, and are but barely mentioned by the
writers of those times [*]. At first, they seem

---

[*] It appears, that the Christians, till the reign of
Trajan, had been so little noticed, that no law had been
established for their trial or punishment. When Pliny
was governor of Pontus, he applied to his friend and
master for instructions how to proceed against them.
The letter is curious, and the answer contains sentiments of justice that do honour to the great man who
wrote it. They are the 97th and 98th in the collection
of Pliny's correspondence.

Tacitus mentions the Christians as having been accused of setting fire to Rome in the reign of Nero. He
says, " Ergo abolendo rumori Nero subdidit reos, et
" quæsitissimis pœnis affecit, quos per flagitia invisos,
" vulgus Christianos appellabat."—And, after having re-
counted the excruciating tortures by which many of that
religion were put to death, he proceeds,—"Ergo quan-
" quam adversus sontes, et novissima exempla meritos,
" miseratio oriebatur, tanquam non utilitate publica, sed
" in sævitiam unius absumerentur." See Tacit. Ann.
Lib. XV.

to have been imprisoned and punished by the magistrates, as men who, according to the then prevailing notions, were blasphemers of the gods. Equally exposed to the aversion of their countrymen and their conquerors, no teachers of any new religion ever began their mission with less apparent probability of success. But, by their confidence in him they worshipped, and their unremitting perseverance, they gradually gained admittance among all ranks of men, from the cottage to the palace. Then, enemies to pride and violence, with the language of persuasion, they taught duties that were agreeable to the soundest principles of morality; they recommended obedience, rather than opposition, to the established government; and by these mild means, their doctrines, in little more than three hundred years after the death of Christ, had made so great a progress, that they were embraced by the Roman Emperor himself. The system of heathen

mythology,

mythology, adorned with all the elegance in its rites that a refined and luxurious people could invent, and which had fo much contributed to the perfection of the arts, fell before the gentle but prevailing force of Chriftianity; and the eagle of Jove, under which the victorious legions had been led, through a feries of ages, to unparalleled renown, was changed for the Crofs, the fymbol of the faith which their fovereign had adopted.

But befides the internal purity of the new doctrine, a variety of combined circumftances contributed to its rapid advancement; and I hope it will not be thought out of place curforily to notice them.

Mr. Gibbon, in his *Hiftory of the Decline and Fall of the Roman Empire,* in following the courfe of human reafoning, and arguing from apparent caufes, has obferved, that the writings of Pagan fceptics had

prepared .

prepared the way, and the doctrine of the immortality of the foul principally contributed, to the fuccefs of the Chriftian religion.

An examination of the writings of the ancients on the fubject of their theology, will fhew that polytheifm was almoft univerfally confidered, by men of learning, as a fable fabricated to amufe the fuperftitious multitude, and calculated to maintain the influence and authority of the prieft-hood. We find that many of the moft celebrated philofophers, both before, during, and after the Auguftan age, made it the fubject of their animadverfion: and as Mr. Gibbon very juftly remarks, the opinions and examples of men eminent for their rank and learning, muft have confiderably influenced the opinions of the people. Few men either take the pains, or are poffeffed of fufficient knowledge, fairly to examine the religion in which they were born; they

in

in general follow it, and believe it prefer-
able to any other, from habit and education.
But when it was known, that those who
held the higheſt ranks in the ſtate, and
who, in conſequence thereof, even officiated
in the prieſthood, in their hearts deſpiſed
thoſe ceremonies which they performed with
apparent ſolemnity; and made devotion,
and the devout, the objects of their wit and
ridicule; others, from vanity, or deference
to their judgment, imitated their example;
reſpect for religion was gradually under-
mined; and the prejudice of education
being removed, the mind, left without any
fixed ſyſtem, lay open to receive new opinions, and to embrace new doctrines.

In tracing the progreſs of a more rational
and pure idea of the Supreme Ruler of the
univerſe, than was entertained from the
earlieſt times by the *many*, we ſhall find,
that the EAST ſhed the firſt light under
whoſe influence the variety of ſyſtems that

afterwards

afterwards prevailed, grew up. Pherecides feems to have been the firft who introduced into Greece a regular notion of
a ftate of rewards and punifhments, in the
doctrine of the metempfychofis, which,
many ages previous to his time, prevailed, not only in Egypt, but among feveral
more Eaftern nations.

Pythagoras*, the difciple of Pherecides,
travelled into Egypt and Chaldea, and, on
his return from Babylon, extended and
improved the doctrines of his predeceffor.
It is a doubt among ancient writers, whe-

---

* Diogenes Laertius, Porphyry, and Jamblichus, who
have written his life, fpeak only of his travels in Chaldea,
Egypt, Greece, and Italy; but from the teftimony of
other authors it appears more than probable, that he
extended his travels to India, and that his philofophical
opinions, and efpecially his doctrine of the tranfmigra-
tion of fouls, were derived from the inftructions of the
Brachmanes. See Eufebii Prep. Evang. cap. 10. 4.
Alex. Polyhift. Apul. S. Clem. of Alexandria.

VOL. I.   C   ther

ther he left any works behind him, or not; but by what may be collected from the writings of his difciples, it appears that he taught the exiftence of a Supreme Being, by whom the univerfe was created, and by whofe providence it is preferved : that the fouls of mankind are emanations of that Being*: that, on their feparation from the body, they go to places deftined for their reception ; the fouls of the virtuous, after having been purified from every propenfity to the things of this world, being re-admitted into the divine fource from whence they flowed ; and the fouls of the wicked fent back to animate other bodies of men or beafts, according to the degree and nature of their vices, until, in a courfe perhaps of many tranfmigrations, they have expiated their crimes. Abftinence from animal food was a natural confequence of thefe doctrines ; but the Pythagoreans re-

---

* See Hindoo Philofophy, SKETCH X.

frained

frained likewife from every fort of intoxicating liquor, and from eating beans, for which
they feem to have entertained a fuperftitious
refpect, though we are unacquainted with
the caufe. Befides theology, Pythagoras is
faid to have inftructed his fcholars in arithmetic, mathematics, natural hiftory, and mufic.
His fchool formed a kind of community,
into which he admitted the women and
children of his followers. He exacted from
his difciples a voluntary poverty; or rather
that they fhould diveft themfelves of property individually, and live upon one common ftock. He impofed fecrecy; and, in
order to teach them patience and perfeverance, they were prohibited from fpeaking
for a greater or lefs fpace of time, as he
thought they ftood in need of trial and exertion*. They were divided into two
claffes.

---

* Some of the ancients, in fpeaking of the education
given to the children of the Brachmanes, fay, that while

the

claffes. Thofe who had made a certain progrefs, were admitted about his perfon, and with them he ufed plain and natural language; but to the reft, who were feparated from him by a curtain, he fpoke in metaphors and fymbols. His doctrines made a confiderable progrefs in Greece and Italy, and probably gave birth to many of the more rational fyftems of philofophy that fucceeded them.

Socrates, who was perhaps the wifeft of all the ancient philofophers, confined his doctrines chiefly tc maxims of morality. He endeavoured to bring men back from the wild and fpeculative notions which

---

the mafters were teaching, the fcholars liftened with filent attention; that they were not only forbidden to fpeak, but even to cough or fpit; that all the fcholars eat in common; that their meals were preceded by bathings and purifications; and that before the firft meal they were obliged to render an account how the morning had been employed. Vide Strabo, 15. Apul. Floridor. 1.

charac-

characterifed the learning of his countrymen at that time, and to confine the ftudies
of his difciples to their own breafts, in which
benevolence and virtue could not fail of
producing happinefs.

His opinions, as handed down to us by
thofe who conftantly attended him, declare
his belief in the unity of God, and in the
immortality of the foul.　He taught, that
though God has not revealed to us, in
what manner he exifts, his power, his
wifdom, and never-ceafing providence, are
exhibited in all we fee: that the order and
harmony which reign throughout the univerfe announce a Supreme Being, by which
every thing is conducted and preferved:
that the religion of every country ordains
his worfhip, let it be in ever fo varied a
manner; and that it is the duty of all
to refpect their national religion, except
in fuch points as may be contrary to the
laws of nature, or may divert the attention

C 3

from

from God to other objects. He seems to have believed that the soul existed before the body *; and that death relieves it from those seeming contrarieties to which it is subject, by its union with our material part. He taught, that the souls of the virtuous return to their former state of happiness, while those of the wicked are doomed to punishments proportionate to their crimes; that happiness, both in this and in a future state of existence, depends on the practice of virtue, and that the basis of virtue is justice. He comprised his idea of virtue in this maxim: " Adore God, " honor your parents, and do good to " all men. Such is the law of nature and " reason." In society, he thought that every private consideration ought to yield

---

* This idea seems evidently to have been borrowed from Pythagoras, who supposed the souls of men to have pre-existed in the divine soul, into which they at last return.

to what could promote the good and safety of the community to which we belong; and notwithstanding the mildness of his disposition, his love of tranquillity, and general good-will to mankind, he entered into the bustle of arms, and served during three years in the Lacedæmonian war, with distinguished reputation. Although he thought it not only weakness, but even impiety, to be afraid of death, he condemned suicide, as a proof of cowardice rather than of courage, and as a desertion of the post assigned to us by Providence. He strongly recommended perseverance, sedateness, and modesty; and of the last of these virtues he was himself a distinguished example, often declaring, that the utmost extent of his researches had only taught him, " that he knew nothing." He opposed the corruption of the magistrates, and the superstition and hypocrisy of the priesthood: and at last fell a victim to their machinations, for practising virtues which

C 4

have

have rendered his name facred to pofterity.'

PLATO, a difciple of Socrates, travelled
into Egypt and Italy *, and upon his return
eftablifhed his fchool at the Academy.
Like Socrates, he believed in the unity of
the Supreme Being, without beginning or
end; but afferted, at the fame time, the
eternity of matter. He taught, that the
elements being mixed together in chaos,
were, by the will of God, feparated, and reduced into order, and that thus the world
was formed: that God infufed into matter
a portion of his divine fpirit †, which ani-
mates and moves it; and that he committed
the care of this world, and the creation of

---

* It appears that Plato once intended to vifit India.
—*Ad Indos et Magos intendiffet animum, nifi eum bella tunc
vetuiffent Afiatica.* Apul. de dogm. Plat.

† This is conformable to the opinions of the learned
Hindoos. See SKETCH X.

mankind,

mankind, to beings who are conftantly fubject to his will. That mankind have two fouls, of feparate and different natures, the one corruptible, the other immortal : That the latter is a portion of the divine fpirit, refides in the brain, and is the fource of reafon : that the former, the mortal foul, is divided into two parts, one of which, refiding in the heart, produces paffions and defires ; the other, between the diaphragm and navel, governs the animal functions : That the mortal foul ceafes to exift with the life of the body, but that the divine foul, no longer clogged by its union with matter, continues its exiftence, either in a ftate of happinefs or punifhment : That the fouls of the virtuous—of thofe whofe actions are guided by their reafon—return after death into the fource from whence they flowed*, while the fouls of thofe who fubmitted to

---

* In this he likewife agrees with the doctrines of the Hindoos.

the

the government of the paffions, after being for a certain time confined to a place deftined for their reception, are fent back to earth, to animate other bodies.

The above idea of a future ftate appears to be the moft prevalent in the works of this philofopher, and to form what may be called his *fyftem:* But at the fame time it muft be confeffed, that he broaches fo many notions of a different or contrary nature, that we are frequently left at large in regard to his real fentiments. A paffion for brilliant and novel doctrines, and too great a defire to acquire fame, even at the expence of truth, feem to have been the caufe of this evident inconfiftency in fo great and wife a man *.

ARISTOTLE,

---

* The learned Monfieur Freret in fpeaking of Plato obferves :

Il dit fi fouvent, et à fi peu de diftance, le pour et le contre lorfqu'il parle de l'etat de l'ame après cette vie,

que

Aristotle, who ftudied at the Academy, has been perhaps unjuftly accufed of ingratitude to Plato.   He undoubtedly ufed the privilege of every philofopher, in advancing his own opinions, and differing from thofe of others, but yet he always admired the talents, and did juftice to the merits of Plato.   He even pronounced an oration in his praife, and erected an altar to his memory.

---

que ceux qui regardent les fentimens de ce philofophe avec refpect, ne peuvent s'empecher d'etre choqués et fcandalifés.   Tantôt il eft de l'opinion de la metempfycofe, tantôt de celle des enfers, et tantôt de toutes les deux il en compofe une troifieme.   Ailleurs il avoit imaginé une maniere de faire revivre les hommes, qui n'a nul rapport avec aucun autre de fes fyftèmes.   Dans un endroit il condamne les fcelerats a refter dans le Tartare pendant toute l'eternité, dans un autre il les en tire au bout de mille ans, pour les faire paffer dans d'autres corps.   En un mot, tout eft traité chez lui d'une maniere problematique, incertaine, peu decidée, et qui laiffe à fes lecteurs un jufte fujet de doubter, qu'il ait été lui-même perfuadé de la verité de ce qu'il avançoit.

Ariftotle

Ariftotle opened his fchool at the Lyceum; and, from his manner of teaching, his difciples became known by the name of Peripatetics. He has by fome been charged with atheifm, but I am at a lofs upon what grounds, as a firm belief in the exiftence of a Supreme Being is clearly afferted by him, and not any where contradicted *.

He taught, that the univerfe, and motion, are eternal, having for ever exifted, and being without end; and that although this world may have undergone, and be ftill fubject to convulfions, yet motion, being

---

* Timéc, Platon, et Ariftote, ont établi formellement l'unité d'un Dieu : et ce n'eft pas en paffant, c'eft dans des ouvrages fuivis, et dans l'expofition de leurs fyftémes fondès fur ce dogme. Ariftote n'a pas hefité a reconnôitre Dieu comme premiere caufe du mouvement, et Platon comme l'unique ordonnateur de l'univers.

Voyage du jeune Anacharfis en Grece.

regular

regular in its operation, brings back the elements into their proper relative fituations, and preferves the whole : that even thefe convulfions have their fource in nature; that the idea of a *Chaos*, or the exiftence of the elements without form or order, is contrary to her laws, which we every where fee eftablifhed, and which, conftantly guiding the principle of motion, muft from eternity have produced, and to eternity preferve, the prefent harmony of the univerfe: that in every thing we are able to difcover a train of *motive* principles, an uninterrupted chain of caufes and effects; and that as nothing can happen without a caufe, the word *chance* is an unmeaning expreffion, employed in fpeaking of effects, of whofe caufes we are ignorant *; that in following this chain we are led up to the primitive caufe, the Supreme Being, the univerfal Soul, who, as

---

* See Hindoo Philofophy, SKETCH X.

the

the will moves the body, moves the whole fyftem of the univerfe: That God, therefore, is the author of nature's laws.—He fuppofed the fouls of mankind to be portions or emanations of the divine fpirit, which at death quit the body, and, like a drop of water falling into the ocean, are abforbed in the divinity. Though he thus admitted the immortality of human fouls, yet, as he did not fuppofe them to exift individually, he confequently denied a future ftate of rewards and punifhments. " Of " all things," fays he, " the moft terrible " is death, after which we have neither to " hope for good, nor to dread evil."

His maxims of morality were of the pureft kind. He taught, that the great end of philofophy is to engage men to do that by choice, which the legiflature would obtain from them by fear: That we fhould honour our parents, love our children, and do good to all men: That focieties, or

ftates, are an aggregation of individual families, bound together by compacts and
laws for their mutual interefts; and that it
is the duty of every member of fociety,
not only to be obedient to thofe laws, but
to neglect no opportunity of contributing
to the general welfare of the fociety or ftate
to which he belongs.

After the death of Ariftotle, the Peripatetics feem to have been divided in their
opinions concerning the foul, fome con-
tinuing to affert that it was a part of the
divine and eternal Spirit; others contend-
ing, that, being united with the body, their
exiftence mutually depended upon one
another, and that both were mortal.

ZENO of Cyprus, the founder of the
Stoic fect, had firft ftudied under Crates the
Cynic, from whom he perhaps imbibed
thofe notions of aufterity which afterwards
characterifed his doctrines.

He

He believed in the unity of the Supreme Being, and that the names of the other deities of his countrymen were only symbols of his different attributes.

He taught, that throughout nature there are two eternal qualities; the one active, the other paffive: That the former is a pure and fubtle æther, the divine fpirit; and that the latter is in itfelf entirely inert, until united with the active principle: That the divine fpirit, acting upon matter, produced fire, air, water, and earth; or feparated the elements from each other: That it cannot however be faid, that God created the world by a voluntary determination, but by the effect of eftablifhed principles, which have ever exifted and will for ever continue: Yet as the divine fpirit is the efficient principle, the world could neither have been formed nor preferved without him, all nature being moved and conducted by him, while nothing can move

or

or affect God : That matter may be divided, meafured, calculated, and formed into innumerable fhapes ; but the divine fpirit is indivifible, infinite, unchangeable, and omniprefent.

He believed that the univerfe, comprehending matter and fpace, is without bounds ; but that the *world* is confined to certain limits, and fufpended in infinite fpace : That the feeds of all things exifted in the primitive elements, and that by means of the efficient principle they were brought forward and animated: That mankind come into the world without any innate ideas, the mind being like a fmooth furface, upon which the objects of nature are gradually engraven by means of the fenfes : That the foul of man being a portion of the *Univerfal Soul*, returns, after death, to its firft fource, where it will remain until the deftruction of the world, a period at which the elements, being once more confounded, will again be reſtored to their preſent ſtate of order and harmony.

Zeno taught, that virtue alone is the ſource of happineſs, and that vice, notwithſtanding the temporary pleaſures that it may afford, is the certain cauſe of pain, anxiety, and wretchedneſs: That as men have it in their power to be virtuous, happineſs may be acquired by all; and that thoſe who by vice and intemperance become miſerable, have no right to complain of their ſufferings: That a virtuous man adores the Supreme Being, reſtrains his paſſions, and enjoys the goods of this world, as if nothing belonged particularly to himſelf; he conſiders all mankind with the ſame degree of affection, and having no ſtrong partialities to individuals, he comforts indiſcriminately thoſe who are afflicted, receives ſuch as want an aſylum, and feeds thoſe who hunger; all this he does undiſturbed by ſtrong emotion; he beholds

the

the divine will in all things, and, amidst the tumults of this world, preserves a mind serene and unruffled! neither reproach nor praise affect him, nor doth he indulge refentment on account of injuries; in retirement, and in the obfcurity of the night, he examines the actions of the day, avows his faults, and endeavours to amend them; and when he finds the hour of diffolution approaching, he is not afraid of death, but either awaits, or voluntarily embraces it.

Thefe feem to have been the principal outlines of the doctrines of Zeno; although many of the Stoics carried the idea of the neceffity of mortification and abftinence to a much greater length, than appears to have been the intention of their founder.

Epicurus, whofe notions were fo oppofite to thofe of the Stoic philofophers, attempted to account for the various operations in nature, without having recourfe to a Su-

preme

preme Being. " There is no occafion," fays he, " to afcribe to the gods what may " be explained by philofophy." But in this bold affertion he betrays only pre- fumption and vanity; as in the place of a rational fyftem, allowing the agency of the divine will, he has fubftituted an hy- pothefis too fanciful and imaginary to fup- port any clear and decided opinion.

He obferves that, before we can form a fit idea of a fubftance that is diftinguifhed by any particular fhape, or that poffeffes any particular qualities, we muft firft have an idea of its primitive conftituent parts. He therefore fuppofes, as the bafis upon which his whole fyftem refts, That every thing is compofed of atoms, differing in fhape, but each indivifible, and poffeffing a natural tendency to unite, the exertion of which is the primary caufe of motion in the whole fyftem of nature, and of the firft formation of all bodies. He fays, that

matter

matter enables us to conceive an idea of certain portions of fpace, as different events do, of time; but it is impoffible to imagine fpace to be bounded by any limits, or time to have had a beginning: That the univerfe muft from eternity have been the fame in its nature, its extent and quantity: That the world—our fyftem—has its limits, and is fufpended in infinite fpace, in which myriads of other worlds may likewife exift: That when we confine our ideas to the world we inhabit, we may form diftinct notions of its duration, and fuppofe it to have a beginning and an end; but if we extend them to the univerfe, and to eternity, we find no refting-place, and they muft neceffarily be loft and confounded in the contemplation: That nothing can be properly faid to be annihilated, for though things may be diffolved from their particular forms, and their component parts feparated, their atoms remain what they

were

were from eternity, their quantity being liable neither to increafe nor diminution.

He fuppofes the foul of man to be likewife compofed of atoms *indefcribably* fmall, igneous, and volatile: That the principal feat of it is in the heart, and that in it originate pleafure, pain, fear, and anger: That it is moved to action by the objects conveyed to it by the fenfes, its chief affections being pain and pleafure, whence arife averfion and defire: That the foul being engendered with the body, grows up and declines with it; that their mutual faculties depend upon their union; and upon their feparation, action being at an end, thought and memory ceafe.

A total difbelief in a ftate of future rewards and punifhments, was the natural confequence of thefe dogmas. Epicurus thought the notions entertained in this re-

fpect

ſpect by his countrymen, of Tartarus, of Elyſian fields, and of a future judge of human actions, very unworthy of philo- ſophy, and unneceſſary to our happineſs. He taught, that the ſtudy of nature, and of her laws, will produce tranquillity and peace, undiſturbed by vain and imaginary terrors: That we muſt not however expect to be perfectly happy; *we are men, and not gods*, and ſhould be contented with that degree of happineſs our imperfect being will admit of: that nature doth not require to be corrected, but to be guided: that happineſs and pleaſure are ſynony- mous; and that the practice of virtue af- fords the higheſt and moſt permanent happineſs, which alone poſſeſſes this pe- culiar property, that it may be conſtantly enjoyed: that the good of ſociety, and the love of mankind in general, ought to direct all our actions: that he who practiſes any one virtue to exceſs, neglecting his other duties, cannot be properly called

D 4

virtu-

virtuous;—our actions muſt be in harmony; the muſician does not content himſelf with tuning one particular ſtring, all
the tones muſt be in concord: that we may
freely indulge thoſe pleaſures, that are not
likely to produce any ill; and that a temporary ill muſt be ſuffered, in order to
enſure a greater and more laſting pleaſure;
but that it is the exceſs of weakneſs to yield
to the temptation of any gratification, which
may leave a greater or more permanent
evil behind: That, to preſerve to ourſelves
the power of enjoying ſenſual pleaſures, we
ought to be temperate in the uſe of them:
That among civilized nations, men, actu-
ated by the public good, ought to be decent in their conduct; and ſcrupulouſly
obſerve ſuch rules and cuſtoms as are eſtabliſhed to preſerve order and harmony in
the community to which they belong.

The doctrines of Epicurus were ſo po-
pular, that the Athenians erected a ſtatue to

his

his memory; they made a very rapid progrefs, and were foon carried into Italy. They were greatly admired by the Romans, and fuited perhaps the feelings of a refined and luxuricus people better than thofe of Zeno. Lucretius, Celfus, Pliny the elder, Lucan, and many other diftinguifhed Roman names, may be reckoned in the lift of Epicureans; and the friend of Cicero, Pomponius Atticus, was a difciple of the Epicurean Zeno of Sidon.

Such are the chief features of thofe doctrines in philofophy which from the bofom of Athens fpread themfelves over Greece and Italy, and at laft found their way into the remoteft parts of the Roman empire. Though feveral Greeks had written in favour of atheifm, yet it feems to have made but little progrefs: even moft of the Epicureans fo far modified the original tenets of the fect as to acknowledge the exiftence of a Supreme Being; and upon

the

the whole we may venture to conclude, that, towards the time of the appearance of Chrift, men of learning, in general, were *deifts*, and that only the people, and the ignorant, retained any refpect for the ancient theology.

But however unanimous they may have been in their belief of the exiftence and unity of one Supreme Being, they were exceedingly divided in their fentiments concerning the nature and immortality of the foul*. Many of the moft eminent philofophers treated the idea of a future ftate as

a fable,

---

* Plato dixit animam effentiam fe moventem; Xenocrates numerum fe moventem; Ariftoteles, intellectum feu motum perpetuum; Pythagoras et Philolaus, harmoniam; Poffidonius, ideam; Afclepiades, quinque fenfuum exercitium fibi confonum; Hippocrates, fpiritum tenuem per omne corpus diffufum; Heraclitus Ponticus, lucem; Heraclitus Phyficus, fcintillam ftellaris effentiæ; Zenon, concretum corpori fpiritum; Democritus, fpiritum infertum atomis; Critolaus Peripateticus, conftare eam de quinta efientia; Hipparchus,

ignem;

a fable, and thofe who profeffed to believe
in it, difagreed fo widely among themfelves, that no clear and decided opinion
can be collected from their works. We
find it a common maxim, that thofe could
not fuffer, who did not exift; and, taking
confolation from an idea, from which nature
recoils, they compared death to a profound
fleep, undifturbed by dreams, when we are
unconfcious of exiftence. Innumerable inftances might be quoted, of the prevalence
of thefe doubts among the philofophers
that flourifhed fhortly before, and foon
after, the appearance of the chriftian doctrines.—A few, however, may fuffice.

When Cæfar pleaded for fome of thofe
that were engaged in the confpiracy of

---

ignem; Anaximenes, aëra; Empedocles et Critias,
fanguinem; Parmenides, ex terrâ et igne; Xenophanes, ex terrâ et aquâ; Epicurus, fpeciem ex igne
& aere & fpiritu mixtam.

MACROBIUS *in Som. Scip. lib.* 1. *cap.* 14.

Catiline,

Catiline, he faid, " that death was not, in
" fact, any punifhment, as it put an end to
" thought and pain."

Even Cicero, after having fhewn the
errors and uncertainty of thofe who had
treated of a future ftate, fays, in an epiftle
to Torquatus, that " death puts an end to
" thought and fentiment;" in one to Te-
rentius, " that death is the end of every
" thing:" in another place, that " a firm and
" elevated mind is free from care and un-
" eafinefs, and defpifes death, which only
" places us in the ftate in which we lay be-
" fore we were born:" and publicly before
the judges and people he afferted, that, " by
" death, we lofe all fenfe of pain*."

Epictetus

---

* Nam nunc quidem, quid tandem illi mali mors
attulit ? Nifi forte ineptiis et fabulis ducimur, ut ex-
iftimemus illum apud inferos impiorum fupplicia per-
ferre, ac plures illic offendiffe inimicos, quàm hic
reliquiffe : a focrus, ab uxorum, a fratris, a liberum
poenis, actum effe præcipitem in fceleratorum fedem

atque

Epictetus was of opinion, that after death we shall return to the source from whence we came, and be united with our primitive elements.

Strabo, in speaking of the Brachmanes, says, " Texere etiam fabulas quafdam, " quemadmodum Plato, de immortalitate " animæ, et de judiciis quæ apud inferos " fiunt, et alia hujufmodi non pauca." STRABO, *lib.* xv.

Seneca writes in a letter to Marcia: " Cogita nullis defunctos malis affici illam " quæ nobis inferos faciunt terribiles, " fabulam effe, nullas imminere mortuis " tenebras nec carcerem, nec flumina fla-

---

atque regionem, quæ fi falfa funt, *id quod omnes intel-* *ligunt,* quid ei tandem aliud mors eripuit, præter fen- fum doloris.　　　　　　　　CICERO *pro Cluent.*

Yet Cicero fays, in another place, " *Naturam ipfam de-* *immortalitate animorum agere, quod fi omnium confenfus* *naturæ vox eft, &c.*"　　　　　CIC. *Tufc. qu.* I.

" grantia

" grantia igne, nec oblivionis amnem, nec
" tribunalia et reos.   Luferunt ista poetæ,
" et vanis nos agitavere terroribus.   Mors
" omnium dolorum et folutio eft et finis,
" ultra quam mala noftra non exeunt, quæ
" nos in illam tranquillitatem, in qua ante-
" quam nafceremur jacuimus reponit.   Si
" mortuorum aliquis miferetur cur et non
" natorum mifereatur." SENECA, *de Confol.
ad Marciam, cap. 19.

The fame philofopher in one of his tra-
gedies, publicly exhibited before the people,
avows the fame opinion*.

---

* Verum eft? an timidos fabula decipit?
  Umbras corporibus vivere conditis?
  An toti morimur, nullaque pars manet noftri?
    S. Poft mortem nihil eft, ipfaque mors nihil:
  Velocis fpatii meta noviffima.
  Spem ponant avidi, foliciti metum
  Quæris quo jaceas poft obitum loco?
  Quo non nata jacent. ——
  Mors individua eft, noxia corpori
  Nec parcens animæ.   *Troad. Aɛ̃ II. Chorus.*

The

The ſentiments of Pliny are very plainly expreſſed in the following paſſage : " Om-
" nibus a ſuprema die eadem, quæ ante
" primum, nec magis a morte ſenſus ullus,
" aut corporis, aut animæ, quam ante
" natalem. Eadem enim vanitas in fu-
" turum etiam ſe propagat, et in mortis
" quoque tempora ipſa ſibi vitam mentitur,
" alias immortalitatem animæ, alias tranſ-
" figurationem, alias ſenſum inferis dando,
" & manes colendo :—ceu vera ullo modo
" ſpirandi ratio homini a ceteris animalibus
" diſtet."   PLIN. *Hiſt. lib. 7. cap.* 56.

Many other inſtances might be adduced, to prove that the belief of the mortality of the ſoul was very prevalent ; and that the notions of thoſe who profeſſed a contrary opinion were often contradictory and con-fuſed, and always without rational proof. Yet every one who reflected, muſt have been conſcious of an intelligent principle within him, anxious to explore this im-

portant

portant but impenetrable fecret, and in fome meafure intuitively convinced of a fuperiority to its prefent ftate, and of an exiftence in another. But though the confcioufnefs of fuch a principle, and the variety of reafons it could difcover to prove its immortality, might lead him to believe it; other arguments muft have offered doubt—he faw the mortal frame conftantly expofed to danger, natural diffolution gradually approaching, and even the faculties of the mind partaking of the decay of the body—he faw the friend that he cherifhed, or the object that he loved, confumed to afhes, or expofed to more humiliating corruption.—Did they exift who were gone?—Was he yet to fee them?—Was he to exift himfelf?—Or was the fcene to be eternally clofed, and all our affections, and thofe mental powers on which we vainly pride ourfelves, to be diffolved in nothing? A variety of anxious thoughts muft have preffed upon the mind; and, in

the

the impatience of agonizing doubt, it was perhaps difpofed to arraign the juftice of the Supreme Being, for having given faculties to inquire into that awful queftion, yet infufficient to refolve it.

In the midft of this folicitude, Chriftianity was announced, declaring the veil which covered that myftery to be removed, and, out of compaffion to the human race, the certainty of a future ftate to be revealed by God himfelf. The pleafing profpect was held out to all claffes of men indifferently; no diftinction was made between the emperor and the flave; happinefs and mifery depended on the firmnefs of belief in the doctrines, and the practice of the injunctions, of Chrift, the morality of which, though confonant to, perhaps furpaffed in purity, the precepts of thofe wife and virtuous philofophers who had already inftructed mankind.

Not lefs flattering than the profpect of the immortality of the foul, was that of the re-

 furrection

furrection of the body; and this doctrine may likewife have confiderably affifted the rapid advancement of Chriftianity*. It was better adapted to the capacities of the illiterate, than the abftrufe notions of the heathen philofophers, and was acceptable to the feelings of all. Such is our dread of diffolution, that even thofe who were not decidedly convinced of the certainty, were flattered with the idea, of a future ftate, where they were again to appear in the form they then enjoyed, and fee and converfe with thofe they loved, in the fhape they had already known them.

The greateft difficulty in the way of converfion, feems to have been the myftery by

---

* Though the belief of the refurrection of the body was profeffed by all the Jews, except the Sadducees, it does not feem to have been entertained by any of the Greeks and Romans.—Many of the Jews, after their return from Chaldea, believed in the Metempfychofis.

which

which God had conveyed his will to man, which being above human comprehen-sion, could not be explained, and was therefore either to be rejected or believed; but, in rejecting this myſtery, men muſt alſo have rejected the authority on which their expectation of a future ſtate was founded.

The early Chriſtians ſupported their faith with great purity of manners; which, with the examples of the martyrs, muſt have greatly contributed to obtain belief, and to ſupply the place of argument. The mind is naturally diſpoſed to compaſſion-ate thoſe who ſuffer; their words and actions have more than ordinary weight. The martyrs ſubmitted to all the torments which cruelty could invent, with patience and reſignation; rejected every offer of re-lief, when propoſed to them on condition of their denying their faith in Chriſt: they met death itſelf with indifference, and in

their

their laſt moments ſhewed the fulleſt per-
ſuaſion, that they were only going to quit a
mortal and inconvenient frame, to enjoy
more perfect happineſs.

That the abovementioned cauſes forward-
ed the ſucceſs of Chriſtianity, may be ob-
ſerved from the little progreſs it has made
in Hindoſtan. The Hindoos reſpect their
own religion, believe in a future ſtate, and
perſecution is entirely contrary to their
doctrines. Notwithſtanding the labours of
miſſionaries, therefore, for upwards of two
centuries, and the eſtabliſhments of different
Chriſtian nations, who ſupport and protect
them, out of at leaſt thirty millions of Hindoos, that are in the poſſeſſions of the
Engliſh and of the Princes who are de-
pendant on them, there are not, perhaps,
above twelve thouſand Chriſtians, and thoſe
almoſt entirely *Chandalahs*, or outcaſts *.

The

---

* " Tout Indien, qui embraſſe le Chriſtianiſme, eſt
" abſolument banni de ſa tribu, eſt abandonné aux
" inſultes

The early Chriftians feem to have been without any fettled hierarchy, and without any eftablifhed forms of religious worfhip. Difperfed in the different cities of the Roman empire, they formed themfelves into focieties, which were only connected with each other by profeffing the fame belief, and being expofed to equal danger.   When the members of thefe focieties occafionally met together, any one fpoke who felt himfelf fo difpofed ; and the firft appearance of diftinction or precedence we can find, was the chufing of prefbyters or elders, to whom was entrufted the care of affembling the members at fit times ; of watching over their manners ; and of affifting their diftreffed brethren from the voluntary contributions of the fociety.   As the number

---

" infultes de toute fa nation : Auffi ne trouvent-on
" point que la religion Chretienne ait fait de grands
" progrés en ce pais la, quoiqu'-en difent les miffion-
" naires Romains."

La Croze, tome ii. *liv.* 6. *p.* 296. *Ed. de la Haye,* 1758.

of profelytes increafed, further and more permanent regulations were thought necef-fary; and the next ftep to higher prefer-ment that is recorded, was the election of certain perfons among the prefbyters, to prefide at the affemblies, to collect the re-fult of their deliberations, and who, in the interim of their meetings, had the power of receiving and applying alms, and of cor-refponding with the focieties eftablifhed in other places. The name given to thefe was *Epifcopi*, a term we find equally applied to perfons in different trufts, and which literally fignified an infpector or fuperintendant *. In the procefs of time, the functions of religious worfhip were entirely commit-ted to thofe infpectors and to their inferior

---

* The title of Pope *(Papa)* was originally given indifcriminately to all bifhops and patriarchs, and it was only towards the end of the 11th century that Gregory the VIIth obtained, at a council held at Rome, that this appellation fhould be confined to that fee. In the Greek church the ancient mode continues to this day.

affiftants;

affiftants; and hence arofe the diftinction of the *clergy*, from the *laity*, or great bulk of the Chriftians. With the augmentation of the number and quality of the Chriftians, the fituation of the clergy became naturally more important; frefh ceremonies were gradually introduced, to render the worfhip more fplendid. From the fuppofed examples in the early ages of Chriftianity, and by forced interpretations of the facred writings, a variety of pious duties was invented, of little real ufe perhaps to mankind, but calculated to obtain and preferve that dominion of the priefthood, by which it fo long kept every other order of men in a ftate of the moft abject fubjection.—It was the flavery of the mind.—Philofophy and the arts, which had already been con-fiderably affected by the influence of the new religion, were loft under the inunda-tions of barbarians that overwhelmed the Roman empire. The fmall degree of un-couth learning which yet remained, being

E 4

entirely

entirely in poffeffion of the priefts, confiderably contributed to confirm their
influence over the rude and uninftructed
laity, and to maintain and extend fuperftition, which, from the earlieft times, they
feem to have foftered with unwearied
pains. Their afcendency being eftablifhed
without oppofition or control, they not
only commanded in fpiritual matters, but
directed in worldly affairs with imperious
interference. Intoxicated with the fubmiffion that was every where fhewn to them,
they often committed fuch wanton and
extravagant acts of authority, that we
are frequently loft in amazement, between
the infolence of thofe who commanded,
and the folly of thofe who obeyed.
But in the plenitude of their power,
and in the enjoyment of the immenfe
wealth they had by various means acquired, they neglected to obferve that exterior decorum with which their conduct
had been formerly clothed, and furnifhed

examples

examples of very licentious and disorderly manners. These did not escape observation; the people in some countries, notwithstanding their infatuation, began to murmur; while the higher ranks of men were already disposed to resistance. The invention of printing, about the middle of the fifteenth century, brought forth science from its dark retreats within the walls of monasteries, from whence it had shed but a faint and partial light upon the universal barbarism of the age. Superstition declined, in proportion to the progress made by letters; phænomena, that had been employed to awe the ignorant, were found to proceed from natural causes; and the minds of every class of men imbibed some part of that knowledge, which now began to diffuse itself all over Europe.

Controversy seems to have been the constant companion of religion:—it was almost coëval with our faith. But early in the sixteenth century it broke out with uncommon violence; and the disputes of church-

men

men were carried on with fo much acri-
mony and imprudence, that by means of
the prefs, the whole arcana of the policy
and abufes of the priefthood were laid
open to the inquiry and judgment of
the laity.

In order to crufh the new opinions,
which, in confequence of thefe difputes, began to appear and to fpread themfelves in
many parts of Europe, the Roman pontiff
had recourfe to violent and injudicious
meafures. Anathemas and excommunica-
tions were pronounced againft all who encouraged or profeffed them; and the princes
of Chriftendom were called upon to exert
their power and authority to eradicate and
deftroy them. But, as is generally the cafe
when perfecution is employed to oppofe
reafon, it decided thofe who were waver-
ing, and made men more pofitive in
their refiftance. The proteftant doctrines
fpread with uncommon rapidity, and operated, wherever they gained ground, not

only

only to effect ecclefiaftical, but likewife the moft important political, changes. During the ftruggle that preceded them, Europe, for a long fpace of time, exhibited the moft extraordinary and melancholy fcene that is to be found in the hiftory of mankind: a ftate of religious frenzy univerfally prevailed. The fire of perfecution was lighted up from one extremity of Chriftendom to the other; and men faw their fellow-creatures and citizens committed to the flames, not only without remorfe, but with pleafure and exultation. All the bonds of focial life were broken; and bigotry and fanaticifm were bufily employed to fmother the feelings of nature, and the fentiments of loyalty, of gratitude, and of friendfhip. Sovereigns defcended from the throne to be the bloody affaffins of their people *, or drove them to abandon

their

---

* Fifty thoufand inhabitants of the Low Countries are fuppofed to have been put to death on account of

their

their own, and seek refuge in other, countries. Confidence and safety were nowhere to be found; for neither rank nor merit, obligations conferred, nor connections of blood, afforded any security. The oftensible cause of these enormities was religion, while the real and true objects of religion were forgotten. Men, apparently deprived of their reason, in the wild course of their mistaken zeal, never stopped to recollect that they were acting in disobedience to the laws of that God whom they pretended to serve, and in opposition to the doctrines they affected to profess, which inculcate charity, benevolence, compassion, and indulgence for the errors and infirmities of others.

---

their religious principles, during the reign of Charles V. only. The number seems almost incredible, but it is affirmed by several cotemporary historians. Yet Charles was milder and less bigotted than his son and successor Philip. The massacre in the night of St. Bartholomew at Paris, and similar scenes of horror in different parts of Europe, shew to what length a blind zeal can carry an unenlightened people.

But

But the charm, that formerly rendered the minds of men capable of receiving with reverence any dogma that was prescribed to them, being broken, every one who was so inclined, commented upon and explained the sacred writings according to his own particular notions: and from among the Reformers arose a variety of sects, as intolerant towards each other, as the church of Rome was towards those who had emancipated themselves from its authority. The laity, who hitherto had been kept in profound ignorance, especially on religious matters, eagerly read the books of controversy, and felt their vanity considerably flattered, in being at liberty to discuss and give their opinions on subjects which but lately it would have been criminal for them to have inquired into. They became accustomed to study and investigation. The liberty that was given to the press in the countries where the Protestant religion prevailed, and especially in those which en-

joyed

joyed a free government, enabled men of
genius to examine things with freedom,
and to exprefs themfelves without reftraint.
Philofophy and the fciences, even in the
midft of civil and religious revolutions, were
making confiderable progrefs; and thefe,
with the improvements in navigation, which
led to the difcovery of other countries and
other people, tended to expand the mind,
and make men more liberal in their notions.
The increafe of circulating wealth, produced
by the extenfion of commerce, and the gold
and filver that were poured into Europe
from America; the eafy communication
that was eftablifhed between different
countries, and the facility of exchanging
their refpective productions, produced new
and varied wants and pleafures. The
ftudious, the induftrious, and the diffipated
part of mankind, found each fufficient oc-
cupation. The fweets of focial life became
more numerous and refined; public tranquillity was neceffary to the enjoyment of
them;

them; and men grew averse to fierce civil broils, and indifferent about religious contests. But as they unfortunately often proceed from one extreme to the other; as formerly it was the fashion to seek fame by wild and extravagant acts of devotion, so of late years some have imagined that they evince a superiority of genius, by affecting to have no religion. But without entering into the arguments either of sceptics or divines, it will always afford comfort to the humble believer, to reflect, that the most profound metaphysicians, the best philosophers of this or any age, and those who have made the greatest progress in the sciences, were not only exemplary in their moral characters, but that their writings tend, while they enlighten the mind, to increase our veneration for the Supreme Being. The farther they proceeded in their discoveries, the more they adored the Creator of the universe, and perceived the

insufinfufficiency of human wifdom to find out or explain his ways.

In fome more modern writers we find the power of fancy, and the force of ridicule, · employed to deprive mankind of their greateft confolation, and fociety of its beft fupport ;—but to what other motive can this endeavour be afcribed, than to a licentious vanity courting a criminal diftinction?

Many of the early Chriftians, even fome of the fathers of the church, previous to their converfion to Chriftianity, had adopted the opinions of Plato, and other Greek philofophers; and hence, doubtlefs, it arofe, that fome of the doctrines then profeffed are evidently tinged with their notions.

The belief of three ftates after this life, which is ftill enjoined by the church of

Rome,

Rome, feems to have been taken from Plato ; but this, as well as other opinions, might probably be traced to a more diftant origin.

The doctrine of the Metempfychofis was openly avowed by fome of the early fects *, who brought paffages from the holy fcriptures in fupport of their extraordinary fictions.

They likewife believed in the eternity of matter, *not fuppofing that any thing could be formed from nothing*. Nam et quidam infirmiores hoc prius credere de materiâ potius fub-jacenti volunt, ab illo univerfitatem deductam, fecundum philofophos †.

---

* See Letter from Father Bouchet to M. Huet Bifhop of Avranches.—Lettres edif. & curieufes, tome xii. p. 170. Edit. de Paris, 1781.

† Tertul. de Refur. Carn. c. 91.

VOL. I.   F   Moft

Moſt of the Gnoſtics imagined that the Divinity (Demiurgus) who created the world, was different from, but ſubordinate to, the Supreme Ruler of the univerſe *.

Origen, and others, believed in the deſtruction and ſucceſſion of worlds; and that theſe revolutions had ever exiſted and would continue throughout eternity †.

This opinion, as well as that of many of the Greeks on this ſubject, ſeems to be derived from the doctrine of tranſmigration; the ſoul that is ſaid to pervade the globe, being ſuppoſed to be infuſed into that which may ſucceed it.—The Origeniſts thought that the ſouls of mankind had exiſted before the body, and, like the Hindoos, rejected the idea of eternal puniſhment.

---

* Ap. Eu. Præp. Ev. xi. 18.

† Orig. in Proem. &c.

Lactantius,

Lactantius, who was selected to be the preceptor of the son of Constantine, and for his eloquence was distinguished by the appellation of *the Christian Cicero*, likewise believed in the pre-existence of the soul *.

The opinion of its being an emanation of the Divinity, which is believed by the Hindoos, and was professed by the Greeks, seems likewise to have been adopted by the Christians. Macrobius observes, *Animarum originem manare de cælo, inter rectè philosophantes indubitatæ constat esse fidei* †.—Saint Justin says, the soul is incorruptible, because it emanates from God ‡: and his disciple, Tatianus the Assyrian, observes, that man having received a portion of the Divinity is immortal as God is §.

* * *

* Lactant. Div. Inst. vii. 5.
† Macr. in Som. Scip. i. 9.
‡ S. Jus. de Resur. 9.
§ Tatian. cent. Grec. N. 10.

Many

Many believed that the Deity had confided the care of the things of this world to
celeftial beings, deftined to that purpofe.
Saint Juftin Martyr fays, in his Second
Apology to the Senate of Rome, " God
" who created the univerfe, having arranged
" the elements, and the fun, the moon, and
" the ftars; having difpofed the feafons, and
" their various productions; having placed
" under man the things of the earth; com-
" mitted the human race, and all that is un-
" der heaven, to angels, whom he has com-
" manded conftantly to watch over them *."

Athenagoras, in an addrefs to the Emperor Marcus Aurelius, obferves, " The
" Chriftians admit of a number of angels
" and fpirits that God the creator diftributed
" over the ftars, the heavens, the world, and
" all that it contains †."

---

* St. Juft. Apol. ii. n. 5.
† Athen. Legat. Chr. n. 10.

Some

Some even imagined, that the ſpace between *the heavens and the earth*, was inhabited by beings that were enemies to mankind, like the evil genii of Greece, and the Deutas of Hindoſtan *.

" All the heretics of the early ages," ſays Father Bouchet, " being infatuated " with Platoniſm, aſcribed to angels, what " that philoſopher ſaid of inferior deities †."

Had we ſufficient data to go upon in examining the hiſtory of the Hindoo religion, we might probably follow the pure worſhip of an almighty, juſt, and merciful God, through all its ſtages of corruption, to its preſent complicated ſtate. The following Sketches may perhaps enable

---

* S. Hier.

† Lettres edif. & cur. tom. xii. p. 191.   Ed. de Paris, 1781.

F 3   the

the reader to form fome judgment upon this fubject; and whatever reafon we may have to confider the religion we profefs as a peculiar revelation of God, we ought to look upon the fincere believers of another, with lefs feverity than men in general have done. To hate or defpife any people, becaufe they do not profefs the fame faith with ourfelves; to judge them illiberally, and arrogantly to condemn them, is, perhaps, in fact, to arraign the wifdom and goodnefs of the Almighty.

SKETCH II.

IN tracing the progrefs of the arts and fciences, we have been accuftomed to confider Egypt as the country which gave them birth; but an opinion has lately been entertained, that they were probably brought thither from Hindoftan. An analogy has been difcovered between the religion of the Hindoos and Egyptians; a fimilarity is found in fome of their cuftoms; and a certain acquaintance with the fame fciences feems to have been common to both. To wreft an honour from the Egyptians which they have fo long and fo peaceably enjoyed, to furmount the prejudices that are in their favour, and to

F 4

over-

overturn an opinion that has been confirmed by the fanction of fo many ages, feems
a work fo replete with difficulty, that I
think no one who fhall attempt it, fhould
flatter himfelf with hopes of complete fuccefs. When opinions are once adopted,
men feldom go fairly in queft of truth;
there is always a bias to thefe; they
generally look for what may ftrengthen,
and receive unwillingly what may combat
them.

In our early youth we imbibed, with claffic
learning, a degree of veneration for the
Egyptians, and hence a predilection in
their favour that will probably remain
with us during our lives. We thought we
beheld the arts and fciences coming from
Egypt, and fpreading themfelves in thofe
countries, to which we always look back
with a degree of enthufiafm; it never entered our imagination to go beyond that,
and to feek their origin in a more diftant
clime; but we gave up our admiration to the

people to whom the Greeks themfelves owed that inftruction which rendered them fuperior to other nations.

From Greek and Roman authors we learn but little of the Hindoos; and the attention they excite in hiftory feems rather to arife from their having been conquered by fome great hero, or mentioned by fome favourite writer, than from their own confequence as a nation. We were indifferent about a people of whom we had fcarcely any knowledge. But the defire of conqueft, and the thirft of gain, having brought us to a more intimate acquaintance with them, and the fpirit of inquiry being roufed, we go back with avidity to thofe paffages which had left but a flight impreffion, and are furprifed to fee the fame manners and cuftoms, the fame religion and laws, exifting, and now in ufe, which we find to have prevailed at the remoteft period we can trace.

Though

Though it be almoſt three centuries ſince Europeans firſt navigated to the Eaſt Indies, it is but a very few years ſince ſuch inquiries were ſet on foot, as could lead us to any ſatisfactory information concerning a people who perhaps merit the attention of the curious, more than any other nation on the globe. But, happily, the obſcurity in which they were involved ſeems gradually to be diſſipating; and we may now flatter ourſelves that we are in the way to obtain a knowledge of all that is to be learnt of their hiſtory. How far that may extend, is yet uncertain; but the lights which have already been obtained, ſufficiently ſhew them to have excelled as a civilized and poliſhed nation, before any other that we are acquainted with.

We are informed that Mr. Haſtings, ſoon after his appointment to the government of Bengal, conceived the idea of procuring a code of the laws and cuſtoms of the Hindoos,

doos, with an intention to conciliate their affections, by paying a proper regard to their inftitutions and prejudices. For this purpofe he invited from Benares, and other parts of the country, Brahmans learned in the Sanfkrit language; the moft authentic materials were collected, and tranflated from the original text into the Perfian idiom. The Brahmans began the work in May 1773, and finifhed it in February 1775 *.

A fociety was fome years afterwards eftablifhed at Calcutta, in order to make inquiries into the civil and natural hiftory, antiquities, fciences, and literature of Afia, which, we are told, has made confiderable progrefs; and that the prefident, Sir William Jones, as well as fome of its other members, are now fufficiently acquainted with the Sanfkrit to be able to tranflate it with facility.

---

* It was tranflated from the Perfian into Englifh by Mr. Halhed.

Of the local ſtate of the country, the beſt account we yet have, is to be found in a *Map* and *Memoir*, publiſhed by Major Rennel, who was ſeveral years ſurveyor-general of Bengal and the other provinces that are ſubject to that government. Be-ſide the ſurveys and inquiries made by Major Rennel and other profeſſional men, our geographical knowledge has been greatly improved, in conſequence of the embaſſies ſent from Calcutta to Thibet and Poonah, and the marches of our armies in the late war with the Mahrattas, acroſs the peninſula from the Ganges to Guzerat. Men of ſcience having accompanied the embaſſy to Poonah, and ſerved in thoſe armies, the preciſe ſituation of particular places, with their directions and diſtances from each other, were accurately aſcer-tained.

I am indebted for much curious, as well as uſeful, information to Lieutenant Colonel Polier, Mr. John Stuart, and Mr. George Foſter.

Fofter. Lieutenant Colonel Polier refided near thirty years in Hindoftan, part of which he fpent at Delhy, and its neighbourhood. Mr. Stuart * and Mr.

Fofter

---

* Mr. Stuart went from Mafulipatam to Hydrobad, the capital of the Nizam's dominions, and from thence to Seringapatam, the capital of Myfore, in which country he remained fourteen months. He came from thence to Madras. In his fecond journey, he went from thence to Hydrobad, Aurengabad, Jynagur, Delhy, through the Panjab, to within fixteen miles of Lahore. He returned to Delhy, and came by the way of Oude and Benares to Calcutta. After remaining fome time in Bengal and Bahar, he went by fea down the Perfian Gulf, and from Ghrey, at the mouth of the Euphrates, croffed the defert in the widest diagonal part to Aleppo, and, embarking at Scandaroon, came to England. In 1783, he went to Mofcow, with the intention of going through Tartary to India, but finding it difficult to procure a paffport for proceeding from Aftracan, he came by the way of Vienna to Italy, and went from thence by fea to Conftantinople. Going by Diarbukkeer (or Mefopotamia), Moful, and Kirkout, to Bagdat, he went from thence into Perfia. After ftaying fome months at Ifpahan, Sheeras, &c. he came to Bafforah, and from thence

through

Foster * have visited more of the interior parts of India than any other Englishman I have heard of; and those gentlemen, by speaking fluently some of the Oriental languages, and by living in habits of intimacy with the natives, have been able to learn things unknown to us, and to explain others which seem to have been misapprehended †.

But the honour is due to the French, of having first brought out, from the recesses of the

---

through Annadolia (or Natolia) to Constantinople and Vienna. He has since then visited Swedish Lapland, above a degree farther north than Torno, and is now prosecuting his travels through other parts of Europe.

* Mr. Foster went from Madras by land to Calcutta, from thence to Benares, Agra, Delhy, &c. to Kathimire, where he continued several months, and going by Cabul through Persia, came by the Caspian Sea to Rullia, and from thence to England.

† Though much miscellaneous information concerning the Hindoos may be found in different authors of our own and other nations, who have written on Hindostan, none that I am acquainted with, have

made

the Hindoo temples, and communicated to the world in a regular and fcientific manner, the aftronomy of the Brahmans, of which, till then, we had but vague and uncertain notions.   It was *Le Voyage dans les Mers de l'Inde*, by Monfieur le Gentil *, that firft enabled us to form a right conception of it, and to perceive thofe characteriftic marks which diftinguifh it from that of

---

made *them* the objects of their immediate and impartial inquiry.   Indeed, until now, the fources of information have been uncertain and confined; but, at prefent, as we have got poffeffion of the key to knowledge, the *Sanfkrit language*, and of the country where its chief repofitory is fuppofed to be, we may expect, from the zeal and abilities of Sir W. Jones, and the other members of the fociety of Calcutta, to have our curiofity gratified, upon better and more authentic grounds.

* See *Voyage dans les Mers de l'Inde*, fait par Ordre du Roi, a l'occafion du Paffage de Venus fur le Difque du Soleil le 6 Juin 1761, et le 3 du même Mois 1769, par Monfieur le Gentil, de l'Academie des Sciences.

other

other nations. Since then, it has been more fully illuſtrated, in a moſt ingenious and learned treatiſe, by Monſieur Bailly *.

Whether the Egyptians received it from the Hindoos, may be a ſubject of farther inquiry; but if, after a careful examination, we are obliged to allow the Hindoos to be the inventors of a ſcience that requires ſo much ingenuity and obſervation, we ſhall be inclined to ſuppoſe that they were likewiſe the authors of that mythology which will be found to bear ſo great a reſemblance to that of the Greeks and Romans.

---

* See *Traitè de l'Aſtronomie Indienne et Orientale*, par Monſieur Bailly, de l'Academie Francoiſe des Inſcriptions et Belles Lettres, des Sciences, &c.

SKETCH III.

Sketch of the History of Hindoſtan.

THE ancient Greeks ſeem in general to have believed that the natives of India were *aborigines* [*], and that they never either emigrated themſelves, or received any colony from ſtrangers [†].

The learned Hindoos ſay, that Hindoſtan [‡], extending from the river Indus

---

[*] Diod. ii.   [†] Strab. xv.

[‡] *Hindoſtan*, ſo called by foreigners; but I am informed that no ſuch words as *Hindoo* or *Hindoſtan* are to be found in Sanſkrit, which we may ſuppoſe to be the original language of that country, or at leaſt the oldeſt now exiſting there. In Sanſkrit it is called

Indus * on the weft, to the Burumpooter †
on the eaft, and from the mountains of
Thibet

Bharata, and *Bharat-virfh.*—Bharat appears, likewife,
to be the name of an ancient imperial family.—
Hindoftan feems, evidently, to come from the Perfians.—*Stan*, in Perfian, fignifies *country*, and *Hindeo*
may have been taken from a corruption of Sinde, the
name of the river that feparated Bharata from the
Perfian dominions. (Rennel—Wilkins—Stuart, &c.)
But to conform to the practice now in ufe, I fhall continue to call the country *Hindoftan*, and its original
inhabitants *Hindoos*.

* From the city of Attuck, in lat. 30. 20. to Moultan.   This river is called Attuck, which in the Sanfkrit language is faid to fignify *Forbidden*, as it was the
boundary of Hindoftan on that fide, and unlawful for
the Hindoos to go beyond it without permiffion.   Below Moultan it is called Soor, until it divides itfelf
into a number of ftreams near Tatta ; the principal
one is called Mehran ; but the river, when generally
fpoken of, is called in the Sanfkrit language Sindhoo,
and vulgarly Sinde.   By Europeans it has, from the
earlieft times, been called Indus.   (Pliny fays, " Indus
" ab incolis appellatus," &c.   Lib. vi.)

† A river eaft of the *Ganga*, or Ganges, the proper
name of which is Brimha-pooter, or the fon of Brimha.
These

Thibet on the north, to the sea on the south ; acknowledged the dominion of one mighty

---

These two rivers derive their sources from the mountains of Thibet, from whence they proceed in opposite directions, the Ganges to the west, and the Burumpooter to the east. The Ganges, after wandering through different valleys, rushes through an opening in the mountains at Hurdwar, and flows, a smooth navigable stream, in a course of about 1350 miles, through the plains of Hindostan to the sea. In its way it receives eleven capital rivers, some of them equal in magnitude to the Rhine. From its arrival on the plains at Hurdwar to the conflux with the Jumna, its bed is in most places about a mile and a quarter wide ; from thence its course becomes more winding : about 600 miles from the sea, its bed in the broadest part is three miles over, in the narrowest half a mile, the stream increasing and decreasing according to the seasons. In the summer months it is fordable in some places above the conflux with the Jumna, but the navigation for small vessels is never entirely interrupted : below the conflux, the depth is much more considerable, as the additional streams add more to that, than to its breadth. At the distance of 500 miles from the sea, the channel is 30 feet deep when the river is at the lowest : but the sudden and great expansion of the

                    stream,

mighty fovereign: but that in this immenfe empire there were feveral here-
ditary

---

ftream, depriving it of fufficient force to fweep away
the fand and mud that is thrown acrofs it by the
ftrong foutherly winds, the principal branch cannot
be entered by large veffels. About 220 miles from
the fea in a ftrait direction, but 300 in following the
windings of the river, the branches called the rivers
Caffembazar and Jellinghy unite, and form the river
Hughly, on which is the port of Calcutta. The navigation of fhips in this river is always dangerous, as
the fand-banks frequently fhift, and fome project fo
far into the fea, that the channels between them cannot be eafily traced. The medium rate of motion of
the Ganges is about three miles, and during the rains,
and while the waters flow into it from the inundated
lands, from five to fix miles an hour. In general,
there is on one fide of the river an almoft perpendicular bank, more or lefs elevated above the ftream according to the quantity of water: near the bank the water is naturally deepeft; on the oppofite fide, as the
bed flopes gradually, the water is fhallow, even at fome
diftance from the margin: but this is the natural
effect of the windings of great rivers, the current being always ftrongeft at the external fide of the curve.

In

ditary kings, who paid him a certain tribute, though in the internal government

---

In places where the ſtream is remarkably rapid, and the ſoil looſe, ſuch tracts of land are ſometimes ſwept away as would aſtoniſh thoſe who have not been accuſtomed to ſee the increaſe and force of ſome rivers, during and immediately after the periodical rains in the tropical regions. The effects of the ſtream at thoſe curves ſometimes produce a gradual change in the courſe of rivers, and in proportion as they encroach on one ſide, they quit the other. Hence there are inſtances in Hindoſtan, of towns, ſaid by ancient authors to be ſituated on the banks of rivers, that are now at a conſiderable diſtance from them. The Hindoos, in their fabulous account of the Ganges, ſay, that it flows from the foot of Viſhnou, the preſerving deity, and in entering Hindoſtan, paſſes through a rock, reſembling the head of their ſacred animal, the cow. The Britiſh nation, with its tributaries, enjoy the whole of its navigable courſe.

The Burumpooter, taking almoſt an oppoſite direction, runs through Thibet, where it is called Sampoo, or Zianciu, which is ſaid to bear the ſame interpretation with the Ganga or Ganges, *the river*. It waſhes the border of the territory of Laſſa, and ap

G 3

proaching

ment of their countries they were independent *.

One of the ancient dynasties of their
emperors is called, the Sourage-buns, or the
dynasty of the children of the sun; the

---

proaching to within about 200 miles of Yunan, the
westernmost province of China, turns suddenly back,
and running through Affam, enters Bengal on the
N. E.   During a course of 400 miles through Bengal,
it so much resembles the Ganges, that a description of
one may serve for both, excepting that, for the last
60 miles before their junction, it forms a stream from
four to five miles wide.   The waters of those great
rivers being joined, form a gulph of confiderable extent, intersperfed with islands, fome of them several
leagues in circumference.   Major RENNEL.

* Diodorus Siculus fays, " India in quatuor latera
distincta est; quod ad orientem, quodve ad meridiem
vergit, magnum mare circumdat.   Quod arctos spectat,
Hæmodus mons ab ea Scythia, quam habitant hi qui
appellantur Sacæ, dividit; quartum, quod est ad oc-
cidentem fluvius Indus terminat, omnium fere, post
Nilum, maximus.   Magnitudinem Indiæ ab oriente ad
occasum, scribunt stadiorum viginti octo millium duo-
rum et triginta.   *Lib.* II. *cap.* x.

other

other the Chander-buns, or that of the children of the moon *.

After these we hear of the house of Bharat: and the wars between two of its branches, the Kooroos and the Pandoos, are the subject of a celebrated epic poem, called the Mahabharat †, said to have been written by Krishna Dwypayen Veiàs, a learned Brahman, above 4000 years ago. A famous battle, fought on the plains of Delhy, at the beginning of the Kaly-Youg, or present age, 3102 years before Chrift, gave, to Arjoon, one of the five fons of Pandoo, and favourite of the god Vifhnou, the empire of Bharatvirfh, or Hindoftan.

---

* The names, however, in Sanfkrit, according to Mr. Wilkins, are properly, *Soory-vangs*, and *Chandra-vangs;* or, *the race of the Sun,* and *the race of the Moon.*

† The Bhag-vat Geeta, which is an epifode of this poem, has been tranflated from the Sanfkrit language into Englifh by Mr. Charles Wilkins. It contains dialogues between Arjoon and Kirfhna, who is fuppofed to have been the god Vifhnou in one of his incarnations.

G 4

About

About 1600 years before Chrift, a war with the Perfians * is recorded; and about 900 years after that war †, another is mentioned, during which the Hindoo emperor is faid to have been carried prifoner into Perfia, and his fon, who fucceeded him, to have become tributary to the kings of that country. The tribute having been withheld by the fecond Phoor, or Porus, is affigned as the caufe of the invafion of India by Alexander ‡. Some Hindoo writers mention the victory obtained by him over Phoor, and fay that he quitted

---

* No mention is made of this war by any ancient European hiftorian.

† The firft Darius, according to Herodotus, invaded India about 504 years before Chrift, which is probably the war here meant. The error in the date, which is about 196 years, may have arifen in copying or tranflating from the Hindoo manufcript.

‡ Pliny fays; "Colliguntur a libero patre ad " Alexandrum magnum, reges eorum ci.iv annis quin- " que millia, ccccii adjiciunt et menfes tres." *Lib.* VI. cap. xvii.

Hindoftan

Hindoſtan on account of a mutiny in his army *.

After the return of Alexander, it appears that ſeveral revolutions happened among the different branches of the reigning family; and that many of the tributary princes, taking advantage of theſe convulſions, rendered themſelves independent. The country thereby lay open to eaſy conqueſt; thoſe princes were un-

---

* This correſponds with the accounts given of the mutiny on the Banks of the Hyphaſis, or modern Beyah. Major Rennel ſuppoſes, that Alexander erected his twelve altars at Firoſepour, near the junction of the Beyah, or Hyphaſis, with the Setlege, or ancient Heſudrus.

It may be mentioned here by the way, that Greek coins, medals, and engravings, are ſometimes found in India. I have ſeen two cameos of exquiſite workmanſhip; and ſaw a beautiful medal of Alexander, about the ſize of a half crown piece, which was given to the Nabob of Arcot. It ſhould be remembered that Alexander had his own coin ſtruck in his army by Greek workmen that he carried with him for that purpoſe.

willing to appeal to a sovereign for protection, whose yoke they had shaken off; and invaders, instead of meeting a united people, and having to contend with the force of the whole empire, seem only to have been separately opposed by those whose territories they attacked.

The Greeks, who remained in possession of some of the northern provinces, were successfully attacked by a Hindoo prince named by them Sandrocottus *. Seleucus, then master of the country between the Indus and Euphrates, made a treaty with him 303 years before Christ; but whether he upon that occasion retained, or ceded, the provinces conquered by Alexander, is extremely doubtful.

About 150 years after this treaty, it appears that some of the same provinces which had been subdued by the Greeks, were conquered by the Bactrians, whose empire

---

* Plutarch.   Justin. lib. xv. cap. iii.

6

was

was formed about 250 years before Chrift, by Theodotus, when governor of Bactriana, under Antiochus Theos. Theodotus was forced to yield his conquefts in India to Mithridates Arfaces king of the Parthians, who confiderably extended them; and the Parthians were in their turn expelled by a Tartar nation, called by Ptolemy and others *Indian Scythians*, who are faid to have fpread themfelves on both fides of the Indus, to the fea [*].

Thefe conquefts, however, may be faid to have extended little farther than the bordering provinces; but the invafions of the Mogul Tartars overturned the Hindoo empire, and, befides the calamities that immediately attend conqueft, fixed on fucceeding generations a lafting train of miferies. They brought along with them the fpirit of a haughty fuperftition; they exacted the converfion of the vanquifhed; and they

---

[*] Strabo.—Juftin.—Excerpta Valefiana.

came

came to conquer, and to remain. The fuccefs of the firft invaders invited many to follow them; but we may confider the expedition of Tamerlane as that which completed the ruin of the Hindoo government. Having, in the year 1398, fent his fon Mirza Pir Mahomed before him, he entered India himfelf; relieved Mirza, who had taken, but was afterwards fhut up in Moultan; defeated the armies of the Mahomedan king of Delhy, and made himfelf mafter of his capital. Wherever he appeared he was victorious; neither Muffulman nor Hindoo could refift his fortune; nor could any one who oppofed him, expect his mercy. Marking the march of his army with blood, from the banks of the Attuck to the eaftern fide of the Ganges, and from thence back by a different route, he returned to Samarcand.

The difappearance of this angry meteor was followed by a long fcene of warfare among the Mahomedan invaders themfelves;

felves; and the firft of the defcendants of Tamerlane who may be faid to have firmly eftablifhed himfelf on the throne of Delhy, was Acbar. He fucceeded his father Homaon in 1556, and died in 1605, after a fuccefsful reign of about fifty years. He confiderably extended the dominion of the Mahomedans, and was the firft of their princes who regularly divided the empire into *Soubadaries,* or viceroyfhips, fome of which were equal in extent to the largeft European kingdoms. Over each of thefe he appointed a foubadar, or viceroy. The foubadaries were again divided into provinces, governed by naibs, or nabobs, who, though fubject to the foubadar, had the privilege of immediately correfponding with the emperor's minifter; the decifion of civil caufes belonged to the Cadi; the revenues and expences were fuperintended by a perfon appointed from the court; and the government of the principal forts was confided to officers who were independent of the viceroy.

During

During his long reign, Acbar caufed inquiries to be made, to afcertain the population, the natural productions, the manufactures, &c. of the different provinces; the refult of which, with various regulations arifing therefrom, were formed into a book called the *Ayin Acbaree,* or inftitutes of Acbar, which ftill exifts in the Perfian language. He endeavoured to correct the ferocity of his countrymen; was indulgent to the religion and cuftoms of the Hindoos; and, wifhing to revive the learning of the Brahmans, which had been perfecuted as profane by the ignorant Mufftis, he ordered the celebrated obfervatory * at Benares to be repaired, invited the Brahmans to return to their ftudies, and affured them of his protection.

---

* Doctor Robertfon fays, this obfervatory was built by Acbar; whereas I have always underftood that it was only repaired by his orders; and hence, probably, it may arife, that the ancient Hindoo architecture is mixed with the pointed Saracen or Gothic arch, which is now to be perceived in the building.

13

The

The dominion of Acbar does not feem to have extended fouth beyond the 21ft degree of latitude. From thence, fouthward, a great part of the country was ftill fubject to a very powerful Hindoo prince, to whom many great Rajahs * paid tribute. The laft of thefe Princes dying without iffue, moft of his territories fubmitted to ufurpers; and two Mahomedans, who had ferved as generals in his army, found means to eftablifh themfelves independent fovereigns of Golcondah and Viziapour.

Aurengzebe, fon of Shaw Gehan, the grandfon of Acbar, completed the conqueft of many countries that his predeceffors had in vain attempted to fubdue. While in the Deckan, he ordered the city of Aurengabad to be built, to commemorate his

---

* Princes, or Nobles, very much refembling the great Nobility of Europe under the feudal governments. *Rajah* is derived from a Sanfkrit word, fignifying *fplendor.*

victories.

victories*.   His dominions, according to Major Rennel, reached from the 10th to the 35th degree of north latitude, and were in some parts, of nearly an equal extent in breadth.   His revenue is calculated to have been about thirty-five millions of pounds sterling :—an astonishing sum, especially in a country where the productions of the earth that are necessary for the support of man, are scarcely above a third of the price that the necessaries of life bear in England †.

Aurengzebe died in 1707, after a reign of forty-nine years ; and though, to attain the throne, he confined his father to his seraglio, caused his brothers to be put to

* His first wife is buried there, to whose memory he erected a mosque, and a magnificent tomb.

† Beside the difference in the price of food, it must be considered that the native of Hindostan has no farther occasion for fuel, than what may be necessary to prepare his temperate meal ; nor for clothing, to guard him against the inclemencies that are unknown in those mild regions.

death,

death, and was guilty of many other enormities; yet, being once eſtabliſhed on it, and ſeeing no competitors, he paid ſuch cloſe attention to the affairs of government and to the impartial adminiſtration of juſtice, was ſo judicious in his political conduct, and ſo ſuccesful in his wars, " that he deſerves to " be ranked with the ableſt princes who " ever reigned in any age or country."

It was the policy of the court of Delhy frequently to change the viceroys. A hiſtorian relates, that one of them left the city, ſitting with his back towards the head of the elephant; and on being aſked the reaſon, replied, "That it was to look out for " his ſucceſſor." The vaſt diſtance of ſome of the provinces from the throne, ſuggeſted the propriety of this meaſure, as well as of the regulations we have mentioned. But, with all the policy that human foreſight might deviſe, ſuch extenſive dominions could only be governed and preſerved, under wiſe and vigorous rulers; and ſuch, when we confider the ordinary courfe of nature, and the ufual education of princes, could not be expected in any long fucceffion. Aurengzebe was a phenomenon that rarely appears in the fphere of royalty: his mind was formed during his long ftruggle for the empire, while he was obliged to command his paffions, and ftudy the ways and cha-racters of mankind. " His fceptre was too " ponderous to be wielded by the feeble " hands of his fucceffors;" and, in lefs than fixty years from his death, his wonder-ful empire was reduced almoft to nothing.

Nizam al Muluc, viceroy of the Deckan, who, without open rebellion, had in reality rendered himfelf independent, to avert the ftorm with which he was threatened from the minifters of Mahomed Shaw, is fuppofed to have fuggefted to *Thamas* Kouli Kawn, who was then at Candahar, his celebrated invafion of Hindoftan.

Thamas, after a fingle battle, entered the city of Delhy, and the vanquifhed emperor

laid

laid his *regalia* at his feet. Having collected immenfe wealth, and referved to
himfelf all the countries belonging to the
Mogul empire that were on the other fide
of the Indus, he reinftated Mahomed Shaw
on the throne with much folemnity, and
returned with his army into Perfia. It is
faid that, before his departure, he informed
the emperor, who the perfons were who
had betrayed him, and gave him much
wholefome advice. But the fabric was
now fhaken to its foundation, the treafury
was empty, the troops were mutinous,
the prince was weak, the minifters were
unfaithful, and the viceroys of the diftant
provinces, though they affected fubmiffion,
no longer refpected commands which they
knew could not be enforced, and in the
end rendered their ftations, that formerly
were of fhort duration, hereditary in their
families. All that now belongs to Shaw
Allum, the prefent nominal emperor, is
the city of Delhy, and a fmall diftrict round
it, where, even deprived of fight by the

H 2

barbarous

barbarous hand of a rebel, he remains an empty ſhadow of royalty, an inſtance of the inſtability of human greatneſs, and of the precarious ſtate of deſpotic governments. Under theſe, while the liberty and life of the ſubject are conſtantly expoſed to danger, the crown totters on the head of the monarch: he who is the moſt abſolute, is frequently the leaſt ſecure; and the annals of Turkey, of Perſia, and of the Mahomedan conquerors of Hindoſtan, teem with tragic ſtories of dethroned and murdered princes.

Throughout Hindoſtan there are many rajahs to be found, who ſtill enjoy the territories of their anceſtors. Some, happily, never were ſubdued, and owe their independence to the natural ſituation of their poſſeſſions, which renders invaſion difficult. Others were permitted, from policy or neceſſity, to retain them, on condition of paying a ſtipulated tribute.

The

The Hindoos are the only cultivators of the land, and the only manufacturers. The Mahomedans who came into India were foldiers, or followers of a camp, and even now are never to be found employed in the labours of hufbandry or the loom.

SKETCH IV.

Government. Public Buildings. Forts, and Places of the Refidence of Rajahs.

THE government throughout Hindoftan feems to have been anciently, as it is at prefent, feudal; and if we may judge from the apparently happy ftate of thofe countries where the deftructive hand of the conqueror had not yet been felt, and from the inviolable attachment which the Hindoos bear to their native princes, we muft conclude, that, under them, they were governed on principles of the moft juft and benevolent policy. In thofe countries the lands were highly cultivated; the towns and their manufactures flourifhed; the villages were compofed of neat and commodious

modious habitations, filled with cheerful inhabitants ; and wherever the eye turned, it beheld marks of the protection of the government, and of the eafe and induftry of the people. Such was Tanjore, and fome other provinces, not many years ago.

Under the ancient Hindoo government, there were feveral kings or *great Rajahs* *, who were tributary to the emperor ; and other inferior Rajahs, or nobles, who paid tribute to their refpective fuperiors, and who, when fummoned to the field, were obliged to attend them, with a certain number of men in arms, in proportion to the value of their poffeffions. Befides the eftates of Rajahs, there were other here-ditary lands belonging to perfons of lefs note, and fome that were appropriated to charitable and religious purpofes. We like-wife find, that in many parts of Hindoftan, certain lands, or commons, were attached

---

* Maha-Rajah.

to

to the different villages, which were cultivated by the joint labours of their inhabitants. The care of thefe lands was committed to the elders of the village, and
their produce applied to maintain the poor,
to defray the expence of feftivals, and to
pay dancers and players, who might occafionally be employed for the amufement
of the villagers.

The *Ryuts*, or peafants, were allowed a
certain portion of the harveft, by the lord
or proprietor of the land, with which they
maintained their families, provided and
kept their cattle, and were furnifhed with
feed for the fucceeding feafon. The portion given to the peafant feems to have
varied, and to have been chiefly determined
by the fertility or barrennefs of the foil, the
eafe or difficulty of cultivation, or the abundance or failure of the harveft.

In countries that are plentifully fupplied
with water, the labour of the hufbandman

is

is much diminished, and his crops are generally very abundant; but on the coast of Coromandel, where the soil is for the most part sandy, and water scarce, greater exertion is required, which is often but scantily repaid.

In such countries as have not the advantage of being watered by confiderable rivers; or in such parts where the water cannot be conveyed from them to the adjacent fields; tanks were made, which, being filled during the periodical rains, furnished water for the rice-fields, and for the cattle in the dry season. Some of these are of great extent, and were made by inclosing deep and low situations with a strong mound of earth *. Others of less magnitude, for the use of temples, towns, or gardens, are of a quadrangular form,

---

* On the bank of the great tanks, are generally found a *Choultry* and a Temple.

lined

lined with ftone, defcending in regular
fteps from the margin to the bottom *.

In the towns, as well as in moft of the
villages, are *Choultries*, or public buildings
for the reception of travellers, which were
erected and endowed by the munificence
of the prince, the generofity of fome rich
individual, or, not uncommonly, in confequence of fome pious vow. A Brahman
refides near, who furnifhes the needy traveller with food, and a mat to lie upon;
and contiguous to them is a tank or well,
that thofe who halt, may have it in their
power to perform their ablutions before
they eat, or proceed on their journey.

---

* I have feen fome of thefe meafuring between 3
and 400 feet on the fide, and regularly lined with
granite. The Hindoos, from fome fuperftitious notion, never conftruct any thing of an exact fquare,
but rather oblong; though the difference is frequently
fo fmall as fcarcely to be perceptible to the eye.

The

The *Dewuls*, or temples, called by the Europeans *Pagodas*, are ftill very numerous, efpecially in the fouthern provinces, and fome of them of fuch remote antiquity, that no account is left, either in writing or by tradition, when or by whom they were erected. But the northern provinces being firft conquered, the feat of the Mahomedan government fixed, and its greateft force exerted in thofe parts; moft of the temples were deftroyed, the images of ftone broken, and thofe of metal melted to cover the floors of the mofques and palaces, that the faithful Muffulman fhould have the fatisfaction daily to trample on what had been held facred by the Hindoo.

The temples at Hurdwar, where the Ganges enters Hindoftan; at Matra, the fuppofed birth-place of Krifhna; at Oudgein; at Benares; and at Jaggernaut on the coaft of Orixa; a temple on the top of a mountain at Trippety, about 40 miles
N. E.

N. E. of Arcot; one on an Iſland called Seringham, which is formed by the rivers Cavery and Coleroon, near Trichanapoly; and one on the iſland of Ramaſſeram, between Ceyloan and the continent, ſeem from the moſt diſtant times to have been conſtantly held in the higheſt veneration. There are alſo many others that are much reſorted to; but of all thoſe of which I have any knowledge, I believe that in Seringham * is the largeſt.

At

---

* About a mile from the weſtern extremity of the iſland of Seringham, and at a ſmall diſtance from the bank of the Coleroon, ſtands this celebrated pagoda. It is compoſed of ſeven ſquare incloſures, one within the other, and ſtanding at 350 feet aſunder. The walls are of ſtone and mortar, and twenty-five feet high: every incloſure has four large gateways, with a high tower over them, one being in the centre of each ſide, and oppoſite to the four cardinal points. The outward gateway to the ſouth is richly ornamented with pillars, ſome of which are ſingle pieces of granite 33 feet long, and 5 in diameter, and thoſe that form

the

At the pagoda of Jaggernaut, people
of all cafts and ranks eat together, without

---

the roof of the gateway, which is flat, are ftill larger.
The pagoda is confecrated to Vifhnou, and in the
inner inclofure are the altars and the image of that
deity. The Brahmans, who belong to the pagoda, are
very numerous, and with their families are faid to
amount to fome thoufands of fouls.

During the ftruggles between the Englifh and French
nations for fuperiority in the Carnatic, and in fupport
of the Mahomedan viceroys, whofe caufe they refpec-
tively efpoufed, the repofe of the Brahmans was difturbed, and their temple profaned ; it was alternately taken
poffeffion of by the French and Englifh armies. When
thefe rude intruders firft attempted to enter it, a Brahman who ftood on the top of the outer gateway, after
having in vain fupplicated them to defift, rather than
be a witnefs of fuch pollution, threw himfelf on the
pavement below, and dafhed out his brains.

About half a mile eaft from this pagoda, is another
called Jumbookifhna. When the French, who, with
their ally Chunda Saib, had been for fome time fhut
up in thofe two pagodas, furrendered them to Mr.
Laurence in June 1752, a thoufand Rajahpout fea-
poys refufed to march out of Seringham until affured
that their conquerors would not pafs beyond the third
inclofure,

out diſtinction or pre-eminence. This
is peculiar to that place, being no where
elſe allowed; and the permiſſion, or rather

---

incloſure, declaring they would die to a man in defend-
ing the paſſage to it: but Mr. Laurence, admiring
their courage, and reſpecting their devotion, far from
giving them offence, ordered that none ſhould go beyond the ſecond.　　　　　　　　　　　ORME, &c.

Tavernier gives the following deſcription of a temple near Amidabad, which the Mahomedans had converted into a moſque : "Il y avoit, en ce lieu là, une
" pagode dont les Mahomedans ſe font mis en poſ-
" ſeſſion pour en faire une moſqué. Avant que d'y
" entrer, on paſſe trois grandes cours, pavées de mar-
" bre, et entourées de galleries, et il n'eſt pas permis
" de mettre le pied dans la troiſieme ſans oter ſes
" ſouliers. Le dedans de la moſqué eſt ornée a la
" moſaique, la plus grande partie etant d'agates de
" diverſes couleurs, qu'on tire des montagnes de
" Cambaya, qui ne ſont qu'à deux journées de là.
" On y voit pluſieurs ſepultures des rois idolatres,
" leſquelles ſont comme autant de petites chapelles
" à la moſaique, avec de petites colonnes de marbre,
" qui ſoutiennent une petite route, dont le ſepulcre
" eſt couvert."

Voyage de Tavernier, tome iii. page 59,
edition de Paris, 1724.

order,

order, for the pilgrims of different cafts to do fo, is faid to be in commemoration of their hero and philofopher Krifhna *, who always recommended complacency and affection for each other. A great quantity of victuals is every day prepared, and, after being placed before the altars, is partaken of by the pilgrims. The Brahmans belonging to this pagoda pretend, that it was built by order of the emperor, at the beginning of the Kaly-Youg †, in honour of Vifhnou, by whom the houfe of Pandoo was peculiarly protected ‡.

There are ruins on the coaft of Coromandel, near Sadras, called, by Europeans, *the feven pagodas*, by the natives, Mavali-

---

* Krifhna is reprefented in the *Mahabarat,* and other works, to be the god Vifhnou in one of his incarnations. See SKETCH III.

† See *Aftronomy of the Hindoos,* SKETCH XI.

‡ See SKETCH III.

puram.

puram. The remains of a palace and temple, of great extent, may yet be traced. Some of the infcriptions and hieroglyphics with which the walls abound, are no longer underftood; and though tradition informs us that this place was at a confiderable diftance from the fhore, many of the ruins are now covered with water, and when it is calm may be feen under it *.

The immenfe temples, hewn out of the folid rock, and containing almoft innumerable pillars, ftatues and figures in bas relief, that are to be feen on the iflands of Salfette and Elephanta, and at Iloura, about 20 miles from Aurengabad †, announce a

---

* There are pieces of fculpture here in very perfect prefervation, which, with many others that are fcattered over Hindoftan, prove the great fuperiority of the ancient Hindoos in this art, to their later defcendants.

† For a particular defcription of thofe temples, fee Thevenot and Anquetil, &c.: but befides thefe, others of a fimilar kind are to be met with in different parts of Hindoftan.

work

work of such astonishing labour, that the people are firmly persuaded it could not have been executed by men, but was performed by genii, at the order of the gods.

The Hindoo poets frequently mention *Duarka* as a place highly celebrated. It is said to have stood at the extremity of the peninsula, and to have been swallowed up by the sea, a few days after the death of Kirshna.

At the hour of public worship, the people are admitted to a peristile, or vestibule, the roof of which, in the large temples, is supported by several rows of pillars; and while the Brahmans pray before the images, and perform their religious ceremonies, the dancing women dance in the court, or under the portico, singing the praises of the god to the sound of various musical instruments.

The inauguration of a temple is attended with great ceremony and propor-

tional

tional expence. After it is completely
finifhed, the Brahmans are perhaps obliged
to wait feveral months, before they find,
by their aftrology, a fit day for that
folemnity. The day is afterwards annually celebrated, and is called *the feaft
of the Dewul.* Every temple is dedicated
to fome particular deity, and each has its
annual feaft; beginning with the day on
which the inauguration was performed:
it lafts ten days, and to temples that are
held in particular veneration, pilgrims
refort on that occafion from almoft every
part of Hindoftan. Few come without
an offering, by which means alone the
revenue of fome of the temples is rendered very confiderable; but, in the countries that are under the Mahomedan
yoke, the Brahmans, as well as the
pilgrims, are ufually taxed by the government.

Throughout Hindoftan we meet with
many places of defence, which, from their
con-

conftruction, as well as from tradition, appear alfo to be of great antiquity, and
feem defigned to refift the effects of time
as well as the attacks of an enemy. Thefe
alone are fufficient to fhew, that the humane laws of Brimha could not fecure the
mild Hindoos from being difturbed by
the fatal effects of ambition; and that the
paffions in every climate are fometimes too
powerful to be reftrained, even by the wifeft
and moft falutary regulations. The building of places of fecurity we find commanded
by the law itfelf; for in the code of Hindoo laws, in a recapitulation of the qualities and things neceffary for *a ruler*, it is
faid, " He fhall erect a ftrong fort in the
" place where he chufes to refide, and fhall
" build a wall on all the four fides, with
" towers and battlements, and fhall enclofe
" it with a ditch, &c."

We likewife find the following paffage
in the Heetopades:

I 2   " What

" What sovereign, whose country is fur-
" nished with strong holds, is subject to
" defeat? The prince of a country without
" strong holds, is as a man who is an outcast
" of his tribe. He should build a castle
" with a large ditch and lofty battle-
" ments, and furnish it with machines for
" raising water, and its situation should be
" in a wood, or upon a hill, and where there
" are springs of fresh water, &c."

Some of those fortresses are by situation
so strong as to baffle all the efforts of
art in a regular attack, and are only to
be reduced by surprise or famine. Such
is the fort now called Dowlatabad near
Aurengabad, Golcondah near to Hydrobad, Gualior *, and many others. But
these

---

* Gaulior, belonging to the Rajah of Ghod, was
taken by surprise by the English in 1780 from the
Mahrattas, who were then in possession of it.

It stands on a rock, about four English miles in
length, of unequal breadth, and nearly flat at the
top. The sides are almost perpendicular in every

part;

thefe feem only to have been intended
by the natives as places of retreat in cafe
of

---

part; for where the rock is not fo naturally, it has
been made fo by art. The height from the plain below
is unequal, but generally from 200 to 300 feet. The
rampart that goes round the top conforms to the edge of
the precipice. The only afcent is by ftone fteps,
which are defended at the bottom by a ·wall and
towers, and in the way up by feven ftrong ftone gateways, at certain diftances from each other. On the
top there are many noble buildings, refervoirs for
water, and even cultivated land. At the north-weft
foot of the mountain is a large and well built town.

Gualior was once in poffeffion of the Mahomedans,
but was recovered by the Hindoos. Tavernier fays,
" Elle (la ville) eft batie le long d'une montagne qui
" vers le haut eft entourée de murailles avec des tours.
" Il y a dans cet enclos quelques étangs que forment
" les pluyés, et ce que l'on y féme eft fuffifant pour
" nourir la garnifon; ce qui fait que cette place eft
" eftimée une des meilleures des Indes. Sur la pente
" de la montagne qui regarde le N. W. Shaw Jehan
" fit batir une maifon de plaifance, d'ou l'on voit toute
" la ville, et qui peut tenir lieu de fortreffe. Au bas de
" cette maifon on voit plufieurs idoles de bas relief·
" taillées dans le roc, les quelles ont toutes la figure de
" demons, et il y en a une entre autres, d'une hauteur
" extraordinaire. Depuis que les rois Mahomedans
" fe font rendus maitres de ce pais-la, cette fortreffe eft

I 3

" le

of need, and for the fecurity of their families and treafures in times of danger; and
not for their ufual refidence, or the defence of the country.

In open and plain countries, the forts
are conftructed with high walls, flanked by
round towers, and are inclofed by a wet or
dry ditch *. The Rajah and his family
generally dwell within the fort, nearly adjoining to which is the pettah, or town.

The

" le lieu ou ils envoyent les princes et grands figneurs
" quand ils veulent s'affurer de leur perfonne."

TAV. tome iii. page 52.

Gualior refembles other forts that I have feen,
being fituated on inacceffible mountains, except by
paffages fecured and defended at different places. On
the fides of the mountain above the paffage, quantities
of ftones are generally to be found piled up, and
ready to be tumbled down on the heads of the affail-
ants.

* I have known inftances of their having aligators
bred in the ditches of their forts, which correfponds
with what Pliny mentions. In fpeaking of the different nations of India he fays, *Horata urbs pulchra,*
foffis

The place of refidence of the Polygar Rajahs, or thofe whofe poffeffions are in woody and hilly countries, is frequently found furrounded with an impervious thicket, clofely planted with bamboos and other thorns.   A road leads from the open country through the thicket to an area in the centre of it, fometimes forming a plain of feveral miles in circumference, on which is the town.   Should it be near to moun-tains, a road fimilar to the other com-municates with them, the entrance to which is commonly defended by a fort, or a deep trench and breaft-work.   Thefe roads are narrow; prolonged by frequent windings, interfected by barriers; and, when an at-tack is apprehended, obftructed, by cutting ditches and felling trees.   By fuch fre-quent interruptions, the progrefs of troops towards the plain is neceffarily flow, during

---

foffis paluftribus munita; per quas crocodili, humani cor-poris avidiffimi, aditum, nifi ponte, non dant. PLIN. lib. vi. cap. 20.

I 4

which

which they are liable to be conftantly annoyed by thofe who may be concealed in the thickets *. Should thefe difficulties

be

---

* The following is a defcription of the attack of one of thefe places, as extracted from a letter of Colonel Fullarton to Lord Macartney and the Council at Madras, contained in his Account of military Operations in the Southern Parts of India, in the Campaigns of 1782, 1783, and 1784:

" On our arrival before the town of Shevigerry,
" he (the Polygar chief) retired to the thickets, near
" four miles deep, in front of his *Comby*, which they
" cover and defend. He manned the whole extent of
" a ftrong embankment, that feparates the wood and
" open country; was joined by other affociated Po-
" lygars, and muftered eight or nine thoufand men in
" arms. Finding that they trifled with our propofals,
" the line was ordered under arms in the morning,
" and orders were given for the attack. It com-
" menced by the Europeans, and four battalions of
" Seapoys, moving againft the embankment which
" covers the wood. The Polygars, in full force, op-
" pofed us, but our troops remained with their fire-
" locks fhouldered, though under a heavy fire, until
" they approached the embankment, where they gave

" a general

be furmounted, the laft refource of thofe
who are attacked, is to retire to the moun-

" a general difcharge and rufhed upon the enemy.
" By the vigour of this advance, we got poffeffion
" of the fummit, and the Polygars took poft on the
" verge of the adjoining wood, difputing every ftep
" with great lofs on both fides. As we found the
" *Comby* could not be approached in front, we pro-
" ceeded to cut a road through impenetrable thickets
" for three miles, to the bafe of the hill that bounds
" the *Comby* on the weft. We continued to cut our
" way under an unabating fire from 8000 Polygars,
" who conftantly preffed upon our advanced party,
" rufhed upon the line of attack, piked the bullocks
" that were dragging the guns, and killed many of
" our people. But thefe attempts were repulfed by
" perfeverance, and before funfet we had opened a
" paffage entirely to the mountain, which is extremely
" high, rocky, and in many places almoft perpen-
" dicular. Having refolved to attack from this un-
" expected quarter, the troops undertook the fer-
" vice, and attained the fummit. The Polygar parties
" pofted to guard that eminence being routed, after
" much firing we defcended on the other fide and
" flanked the *Comby*. The enemy feeing us mafters
" of the mountain, retreated under cover of the
" night by paths inacceffible to regular troops, and we
" took poffeffion of this extraordinary recefs."

tains.

tains. Even the common roads through the *Pollams*, or possessions of these Rajahs, have generally thick woods on each side of them, and gateways or barriers across, which, besides serving as a defence, are intended for the purpose of levying duties on merchandise.

SKETCH V.

Casts, or Tribes.

THE Hindoos are divided into four *casts* or tribes, the *Brahman*, the *Khatry*, the *Bhyse**, and the *Soodera*. These *casts* are at present again separated into two parties, or sects, though we must suppose them to have been originally united. The one is called the Vishnou-Bukht, and the other the Shiva-Bukht, or the followers of Vishnou, and the followers of Shiva. The former distinguish themselves by painting the forehead with a

---

* The name in Sanskrit is, *Visyas;* or, as it is pronounced in some parts, *Bisyas.*

horizontal

horizontal line, and the latter with a perpendicular one *.

Accord-

---

* Beſide the four *caſts* above mentioned, there is
an adventitious tribe or race of people, called in the
Sanſkrit, Chandalas; and on the coaſt of Coromandel, Pariars; who are employed in the meaneſt offices,
and have no reſtrictions with regard to diet. Their
number, compared with that of any other *caſt*, is inconſiderable, and ſeems evidently to conſiſt of thoſe
perſons that have been expelled their *caſts*, which is
a puniſhment inflicted for certain offences. Were a
Hindoo of any of the other *caſts* to touch a Chandala,
even by accident, he muſt waſh himſelf and change
his raiment. He would refrain from the productions
of the earth, if he knew that they had been cultivated
by a Chandala. A Chandala cannot enter a temple,
or be preſent at any religious ceremony. He has no
rank in ſociety, and cannot ſerve in any public em-
ployment. Hence the puniſhment of expulſion, which
is ſuppoſed in its conſequences to extend even to
another life, becomes more terrible than that of
death.

Strabo and Diodorus Siculus erroneouſly divide the
Hindoos into ſeven tribes. Into this miſtake they
have been led by ſuppoſing the Viſhnou-Bukht, and
Shiva-

According to the Hindoo account of the creation, as contained in the facred books, the Veds *, and explained in different Saftras †, Brahma, or God, having commanded the world *to be*, created Bawaney, who, dancing and finging the praifes of the Supreme, dropped from her womb

---

Shiva-Bukht, together with the Chandalas, to be *tribes:* or, by taking for *tribes,* fome of the profeffions into which the Scoderas are divided.

* The Veds, or as pronounced in fome parts of Hindoftan, Beds, and on the coaft of Coromandel, Vedams, contain all the principles of their religion, laws, and government, and are fuppofed to be of divine origin. The Tallinghas, and Malabars or Tamouls, generally change the B into V, and terminate the Sanfkrit words with an M.

† Some of the Saftras are commentaries on the Veds, and have been written by different ancient Pundits. The Neetee Saftra is a fyftem of ethics. The Dharma Saftra treats of religious duties, &c.

Pooran, which we often find mentioned, literally fignifying *ancient*, is a title given to a variety of works which treat of their gods and heroes.

three

three eggs * upon the ground, from which were produced three beings, Brimha, Vishnou, and Shivah. To the first,

---

* In the account given of the birth of those three beings, we may find an analogy with the opinions of some Egyptians and Greeks. The Thebans, in comparing the world to an egg, said that it had come out of the mouth of the Supreme Being *. In the verses ascribed to Orpheus, it is said that God having produced a large egg, and broke it, from thence came out the heavens and the earth †. Pythagoras made use of the same allegory; and we are told, that the *Orphiques*, who pretend to have preserved the doctrines of Pythagoras, abstained from eating eggs, as the Brahmans do now. In the orgies of Bacchus, the egg was consecrated, and held in veneration as a symbol of the world, *and of him who contains every thing within himself.* " Consule initiatos " liberi patris in quibus hac veneratione ovum co- " litur, ut ex formâ tireti ac pené sphærat atque un- " diqueverfum claufâ et includente intra se vitam, " mundi fimulachrum vocatur ‡."

* Eufeb. Præp. Ev. i. 10.—& lib. iii. c. 11.
† Apud. Athenag. legat. pro Chrift. N. 18.
‡ Macrob. Saturn. viii. cap. 16.

5   Brahma

Brahma gave the power of creating the things of this world; to the second, that of cherishing and preserving them; and to the third, that of restraining and correcting them.

Brimha created the Brahman from his mouth: his rank was, therefore, the most eminent; and his busineſs, to perform the rites of religion, and to inſtruct mankind in their duty.

He next created the Khatry from his arms; and his duty was to defend the people, to govern, and to command.

He then created the Bhyſe from his thighs and belly; and his busineſs was to provide, and to ſupply by agriculture and traffic.

The Soodera he created from his feet; and to him devolved the duty to labour, to ſerve, and to obey.

He

He then proceeded to create all other animate and inanimate things; and the Supreme Being infufed into mankind the principles of piety, of juftice, of compaffion, and of love; of luft, of avarice, of pride, and of anger; with underftanding and reafon, to prefide over and apply them.

Brimha having reflected within himfelf, and being infpired by the *principle of wifdom*, wrote rules for the promotion of virtue, and the reftraining of vice; fixed the duties of the Brahman, the Khatry, the Bhyfe, and the Soodera; and calling thefe writings *Veds*, he delivered them to the Brahman, with power to read and to explain them *.

The

---

* " The natural duty of the Brahman is peace, " felf-reftraint, patience, rectitude, wifdom, and " learning."

" The

The Brahmans fhed no blood, nor eat any thing that has had life in it *; their diet is rice and other vegetables, prepared with a kind of butter called ghee †, and with

---

" The natural duties of the Khatry are, bravery,
" glory, not to flee from the field, rectitude, gene-
" rofity, and princely conduct."

" The natural duty of the Bhyfe is, to cultivate the
" land, to tend the.cattle, to buy and fell."

" The natural duty of the Soodera is, fervitude."

" A man being contented with his own particular
" lot and fituation, obtaineth perfection."

" A man by following the duties which are ap-
" pointed by his birth, doeth no wrong."

" A man's own calling ought not to be forfaken."

Bhagvat Geeta.

Only the Brahmans may read the Veds; the Khatries may hear them read; but the other *cofls* may only hear the Saftras, or Commentaries on the Veds.

* Porphiry and Clement of Alexandria, fpeaking of the ancient Brahmans, fay, they drank no wine, nor eat any animal food.

† *Ghee* is butter melted and refined, which, thus prepared, may be kept a confiderable time, even in a hot climate.

VOL. I.   K   ginger

ginger and other fpices; but they confider milk as the pureft food, as coming from the cow, an animal for whofe fpecies they have a facred veneration.

This veneration for the ox may have been ordained, to preferve from flaughter an animal that is of fo great utility to mankind, particularly in Hindoftan, which is productive but of few horfes, comparatively with the extent of the country, and the number of its inhabitants. The veneration in which the ox was held by the Egyptians, may have been borrowed from the Hindoos, or may have arifen from the fame caufe, which may likewife have given birth to *the bull of Zoroafter.* Cicero obferves, that it was the utility of certain animals that occafioned their being worfhipped by the Egyptians and other nations *. Plutarch

---

* " Ipfi, qui irridentur Egyptii, nullam belluam, nifi
" ob aliquam utilitatem quam ex câ caperent confecrave-
" runt,

tarch fays nearly the fame thing*. A fimilar regard feems to have been fhewn for the ox by the Phenicians. Porphiry fays, that a Phenician would fooner eat a piece of human flefh than tafte that of an ox †. In the early ages of Athens it appears, that not only this animal, but all beafts of labour were referved from flaughter, even from being offered in facrifice, and which was one of the laws renewed by Draco.—In the code of Gentoo laws we find, befides preferving the animal from being killed, " that if any one fhall exact labour from " a bullock that is hungry or thirfty, or " oblige him to labour when fatigued or " out of feafon, the magiftrate fhall fine " him."

All Brahmans are not priefts, yet all priefts are Brahmans. Thofe who are not

----

" runt, concludam belluas a barbaris propter beneficium " confecratas." Cic. de Nat. Deor. Lib. I. N. 37.

  * Plut. de Ifid. et Ofir.

  † Porph. de Abft. 11.

of

of the order of the priefthood, whether followers of Vifhnou or of Shiva, may ferve, but not in menial offices; we often find them acting as fecretaries, and superintendants, to perfons of high rank, as factors to bankers and merchants: and there are inftances of Brahmans being firft minifters, not only to Hindoo princes, but even to Mahomedans, being preferred for their knowledge, fobriety of manners, and conftant application. Some even bear arms, but none of thefe can be admitted into the priefthood, and, in their appearance, they are only diftinguifhed from the other Hindoos by the mark on their forehead. They likewife, however, abftain from animal food; and they meet with refpect from the members of the other *cafts*, though not in fo great a degree as the priefts. But thofe who are of the priefthood, confine their attention to the performance of religious ceremonies, to the fervice of the temples, to ftudy, and to the education of youth.

The

The priests never carry weapons of any kind, nor is it suppofed to be fit for them to employ them, even in their own defence. They are patiently to ſubmit to violence, and leave it to God and the laws to avenge them.

But throughout thefe laws, which were moſt probably compofed by the Brahmans, reigns an uncommon degree of partiality to their *caſt*. They claim a pre-eminence in rank, even to their princes, or *rajahs*, who are of the fecond, or Khatry *caſt*. A *rajah* will receive, and tafte with refpect, the food prepared by a Brahman, but a Brahman dare not eat of any thing that may have been touched by one of another *caſt*. In the adminiſtration of juſtice, the puniſhment of a Brahman for any crime is milder, and in general of a lefs difgraceful nature, than that of another man for the fame offence; and they have defcended to the moſt minute circumſtances, in order

K 3

to

to preferve that deference and refpect which they have eftablifhed as their due.

It is faid, in their laws, " If a Brahman " commit a crime deferving of a capital " punifhment, the magiftrate fhall, to " prevent his committing a fimilar crime " in future, fentence him to perpetual im- " prifonment.—There is no crime in the " world fo great as that of murdering a " Brahman; and therefore no magiftrate " fhall ever defire the death of a Brahman, " or cut off one of his limbs.

" Whatever orders fuch Brahmans as " are Pundits fhall deliver to the Ryuts " from the Saftra, the Ryuts fhall ac- " knowledge and obey.

" If a Soodera give much, and fre- " quent, moleftation to a Brahman, the " magiftrate fhall put him to death.

" If

" If a Brahman go to wait on a
" prince, the fervants and *derbans* fhall
" not obftruct his entrance, but give him
" a ready admiffion.

" If a Brahman be paffenger in a boat,
" he fhall not pay any thing to the water-
" man; and he fhall enter and leave the
" boat before any other of the paffen-
" gers," &c.

In fettling precedence, and making way
on the road, all are obliged to yield to the
Brahmans *.

The functions of royalty devolve without exception on the Khatry *caft*; and

---

* Diodorus Siculus, in fpeaking of the cafts
among the Hindoos, fays, " Primum eft philofopho-
" rum qui ceteris, numero pauciores, fupereminent
" dignitate. Ii ab omni opere immunes, neque
" ferviunt cuiquam neque imperant."

Diod. Siculus, Lib. II. *cap.* x.

the

the poffeffions and authority of their *ra-jahs* are hereditary, defcending in the line of legitimate *male* primogeniture. But as the right of blood defcends only to *this* degree, in default thereof the prince may adopt any one of his kinfmen to be his fucceffor *, who, from the time of his adoption, obtains the rights and the appellation of his fon.

The younger branches of the families of rajahs generally ferve in a military capacity, and have fometimes lands given them, which they hold by a feudal tenure.

All commercial tranfactions are committed to the Bhyfe, or Bannian.

---

* Inftances of this kind frequently occur. Viziaram-rauze, the prefent rajah of Vizianagaram, was adopted in preference to his elder brother Sittaram-rauze.

The

The Soodera *cast* is by far more numerous than all the other casts together, and comprises the artisan, and the labourer of every kind. The mechanics and artisans are again divided into as many classes as there are professions. Ninety-eight subdivisions of the different casts have been reckoned by the Danish missionaries, who have given an account of their names, and different employments *. All follow the professions of their fathers. None can quit the class he belongs to, or be admitted, or marry, into another: and hence probably that resemblance that some have pretended to observe in each class, as if composing one great family.

The cheerful resignation of the Soodera to his inferior state in society, with the impossibility of rising above it, besides the effect of education, may be ascribed to the influence of his religion. He is taught by it to be-

---

* De la Croze, Hist. du Christ. des Indes.

lieve

lieve that he is placed in the sphere he now moves in, by way of trial, or for offences committed in a former life, and that by piety and resignation he will enjoy greater happiness in another.

Though the other *casts* enjoy greater liberty with respect to diet than the Brahmans, yet they scrupulously refrain from what is forbidden them, and will not partake of what may have been provided by any of an inferior *cast*, or different religion *.

They

---

* Were a Hindoo to break those rules, he would be expelled from his cast. It having been found requisite to send some regiments of Seapoys from one English settlement to another by sea, those who were Hindoos were permitted to provide and carry with them water and provisions for their own particular use : but one of the ships happening to be longer in the passage than had been expected, nothing remained to them, for several days before their arrival at land, but a very small quantity of dry rice to each daily, without water to dress it, and scarcely more than sufficient to wet their mouths; yet they could not be prevailed on to

taste

They may eat fish and flesh, but not of all kinds indifferently; and to abstain from them is considered a virtue, as may be observed in the following passage of the Heetopades * :

---

taste the other water or provisions that were on board, though almost expiring from thirst and want of nourishment.

* The Heetopades, Heetopadesa, or Apologues of Vishnou-Sarma, an ancient Brahman, was translated from the Sanskrit by Mr. Charles Wilkins, and published in 1787. Mr. Wilkins says, that the meaning of the word is, *useful instruction*. Sir William Jones acquaints us, in a discourse to the society of Calcutta, " That the fables of Vishnou-Sarma, improperly called " the fables of Pilpay, are the most beautiful and an- " cient collection of apologues in the world, and are " now extant under different names in various lan- " guages. That they appear to have been first trans- " lated from the Sanskrit in the sixth century, by " Buzerchumihr, chief physician, and afterwards vizir, " to the great Anushirwan, king of Persia." Mr. Wilkins observes, that the Persian version of Abul Mala Naffer Alla Muftofi, made in the 515th year of the Hegira, was translated into French with the title of *Les conseils et les maximes de Pilpay, philosophe Indien, sur les divers états de la vie;* and that this resembles the original more than any other translation he has seen.

" Those

" Thofe who have forfaken the killing
" of all; thofe whofe houfes are a fanc-
" tuary to all; they are in the way to
" heaven."

No Hindoo of any of the four *cafts* is allowed, by his religion, to tafte any intoxicating liquor; it is only drank by ftrangers, dancers, players, and Chandalahs, or outcafts; and the wine or liquor mentioned by Quintus Curtius we are at a lofs to account for, unlefs it were the *toddy*, or juice of the cocoa, the *palmyra*, and date tree, which, before it be fermented, is of a cooling purgative quality, and drank on that account *.

That

---

* The three fpecies of the palm tree that I have mentioned, are in great abundance over almoft the whole peninfula and iflands of India.

The *cocoa*, which is the firft in rank, is perhaps of more univerfal ufe to man, than any other tree the earth produces. It generally grows almoft perfectly ftraight, is from thirty to forty feet high, and about a

foot

That the Hindoos retain their original character and manners, notwithstanding

---

foot in diameter. It has no branches; but about a dozen leaves spring immediately from the trunk near the top, which are about ten feet long, and, at the bottom of the leaf, from two to three in breadth. These leaves serve to cover the houses of the common classes of the natives, to make mats for them to sit and lie upon; with the finest fibres of the leaf, very beautiful mats are made, that are bought by the rich; the coarse fibres are made into brooms; and the stem of the leaf, which is about as thick as a man's ankle, is used for fuel. The wood of the tree when fresh cut, is spungy; but this, as well as that of the *palmyra* tree, becomes hard by being kept, and attains a dark brown colour.—On the top of the tree, a large shoot is found, which, when boiled, resembles brocalo, but is perhaps of a more delicate taste, and though much liked, is seldom eat by the natives, as, on cutting it, the pith being left exposed, the tree dies. Between this shoot and the leaves spring several buds, from which, on making an incision, distils a juice, differing little either in colour or consistence from water. Men, whose business it is, climb to the tops of the trees in the evening, with earthen pots tied round their waste, which they fix to receive this juice, and take away early in the morning

before

ing the conqueſt of their country by ſtrangers, is owing to the religious obſerv-

---

before the ſun has had any influence on it. The liquor, thus drawn, is generally called *Tary*, and by the Engliſh *Toddy*. It is in this ſtate cooling, and of a ſweet agreeable taſte—after being kept a few hours, it begins to ferment, acquires a ſharper taſte, and a ſlighter intoxicating quality. By boiling it, a coarſe kind of ſugar is made; and by diſtillation it yields a ſtrong ſpirit, which being every where ſold, and at a low price, contributes not a little to ruin the health of our ſoldiers. The name given to this ſpirit by the Engliſh is *Parriar arrack*, as it is drank by the Parriars or outcaſts.—The trees from which the *toddy* is drawn, do not bear any fruit; but if the buds be left entire, they produce cluſters of the *cocoa-nut*. This nut, in the huſk, is full as large as a man's head; and, when once ripe, falls with the leaſt wind.—When freſh gathered it is green on the outſide; the huſk and the ſhell are tender. The ſhell when diveſted of the huſk may be about the ſize of an oſtrich's egg; it is lined with a white pulpy ſubſtance, and contains about a pint, or a pint and a half, of liquor like water, and though the taſte be ſweet and agreeable, it is different from that of the *toddy*.

obſervance of their rules and cuſtoms, from which no hope of advantage, or fear

---

In proportion as the fruit grows old, or is kept, the ſhell hardens, the liquor diminiſhes, and is at laſt entirely abſorbed by the white pulpy ſubſtance, which gradually attains the hardneſs of the kernel of the almond, and is almoſt as eaſily detached from the ſhell. The Indians uſe this nut in their cookery.—From it great quantities of the pureſt and beſt lamp oil is preſſed; and the ſubſtance, after it has been preſſed, ſerves to feed poultry and hogs, and is found an excellent nouriſhment for them. Cups, and a variety of ſmall utenſils, are made of the ſhell.—The huſk is at leaſt an inch in thickneſs, and being compoſed of ſtrong fibres that eaſily ſeparate, it furniſhes all the Indian cordage.

The *palmyra*, or as it is called by the Portugueſe (from whom the Engliſh, as in many other inſtances, have borrowed the name) the *palmeiro-brabo*, is taller than the *cocoa*, greater quantities of toddy are drawn from it; for though a ſmall fruit which it yields be ſometimes eat, and is thought wholeſome, yet it is but little ſought after. This tree, like the *cocoa*, has no branches, but only a few large leaves quite at the top, which are alſo employed to thatch houſes, and to make mats and umbrellas.

fear of punishment, can poffibly engage them to depart.

---

umbrellas. The timber of this tree is much ufed in building.

The *date-tree* is not fo tall as the *cocoa*. The fruit never arrives to maturity in India; toddy is drawn from it, but neither in fuch quantity, nor of fo good a quality, as that which is procured from the two former fpecies. Indeed, the Indian date-tree is but of little value, comparatively with even the *palmyra*, though that be inferior to the cocoa.

Religion of the Hindoos.

WHATEVER opinion may be formed of the Hindoo religion itself, we cannot deny its profeſſors the merit of having adhered to it with a conſtancy unequalled in the hiſtory of any other. The number of thoſe who have been induced or compelled to quit their doctrines, notwithſtanding the long period of their ſubjection, and the perſecutions they have undergone, is too inconſiderable to bear any proportion to the number of thoſe who have adhered to them.

It is a circumſtance very ſingular, and merits particular attention, that, contrary to the practice of every other religious society, the Hindoos, far from disturbing those who are of a different faith, by endeavours to convert them, cannot even admit any proselytes; and that, notwithstanding the exclusion of others, and though tenacious of their own doctrines, they neither hate, nor despise, nor pity, such as are of a different belief, nor do they think them less favoured by the Supreme Being than themselves. They say, that if the Author of the universe preferred one religion to another, *that only* could prevail which he approved; because to suppose such preference, while we see so many different religions, would be the height of impiety, as it would be supposing injustice towards those that he left ignorant of his will; and they therefore conclude, that every religion is peculiarly adapted to the country and people where it is practised, and that all, in their original purity, are equally acceptable to God.

The

The Brahmans *, who tranflated from the Sanfkrit language the laws and cuftoms of the Hindoos, fay, in the preliminary difcourfe prefixed to their work;

" From men of enlightened underftand-
" ings and found judgment, who, in their
" refearches after truth, have fwept away
" from their hearts malice and oppofition,
" it is not concealed that the diverfities of
" belief, which are caufes of enmity and
" envy to the ignorant, are in fact a de-
" monftration of the power of the Supreme
" Being."

" The truly intelligent well know, that
" the difference and variety of created
" things, and the contrarieties of conftitu-
" tions, are types of *his* wonderful attri-
" butes, whofe complete power formed all
" things in the animal, vegetable, and ma-
" terial world; whofe benevolence felected
" man to have dominion and authority over

---

* See SKETCH II.

" the

" the reſt; who, having beſtowed on him
" judgment and underſtanding, gave him
" ſupremacy over the corners of the world;
" who, having put into his hands the con-
" trol and diſpoſal of all things, appointed
" to each nation its own religion; and who
" inſtituted a variety of tribes, and a mul-
" tiplicity of different cuſtoms, but views
" with pleaſure in every place the mode of
" worſhip particularly appointed to it; he
" is with the attendants upon the moſque,
" in counting the ſacred beads; and he is
" in the temple with the Hindoos, at the
" adoration of the idols."

However the intention of thoſe idols may
have been corrupted in a long courſe of
practice by the ignorant multitude, or artful prieſt, they, as well as their various
deities, ſeem evidently to have been only
deſigned to ſhew the attributes of a Being
of whom we cannot form any preciſe or
ſimple idea, and who cannot be repreſented
under any particular ſhape; neither have

they

they any image of Brama *, or God, who
they sometimes call the *Principle of Truth*,
the *Spirit of Wisdom*, the *Supreme Being*, the
Universal Soul that penetrates every thing,
and epithets of the same kind.   They say,
" that the mind may form some conception
" of his attributes, when brought separately
" before it; but who can grasp *the whole*
" within the limited circle of human
" ideas ?

Saint Francis Xavier says, that a Brahman on the coast of Malabar confided to
him, that one of the mysteries or secrets of
the Hindoo doctrines consisted in believing
that there was only one God, creator of the

---

* See SKETCH V. Mr. de la Croze, however,
mentions to have seen a Hindoo painting of *a triangle*,
enclosed in a circle, which was said to be intended as an
emblematical indication of the Supreme Being : but he
observes, that this is not as a thing to worship, and
that no image is ever made of God. Hist. du Christ.
des Indes.

heavens

heavens and the earth, and that only *that God* was worthy to be adored *.

Bernier, who was an attentive traveller, a faithful narrator, and who, if we make allowances for the prejudices of the age in which he lived, may be confidered as a judicious obferver, gives the following account of a converfation he had with fome of the principal *pundits* at Benares, upon the fubject of the worfhip of idols among the Hindoos.

"Lorfque je defcendis le long du Gange,
"et que je paffai par Benares, j'allai trouver
"le chef des Pundets qui fait là fa demeure
"ordinaire. C'eft un religieux tellement
"renommé pour fon favoir, que Chah
"Jehan †, tant pour fa fcience que pour
"complaire aux Rajas, lui fit penfion de

---

* Lib. I. Ep. 5.

† The father of Aurengzebe: his name is generally written by the Englifh, Shaw Jehan.

"deux

" deux mille roupies. C'etoit un gros
" homme, très bien fait, et qu'on re-
" gardoit avec plaifir : pour tout vêtement
" il n'avoit qu'une efpece d'écharpe
" blanche de foye, qui étoit liée à l'entour
" de fa ceinture, et qui pendoit jufqu'à
" mi-jambe, avec un autre écharpe rouge,
" de foye, affez large, qu'il avoit fur fes
" épaules comme un petit manteau. Je
" l'avois vu plufieurs fois à Delhi dans
" cette pofture, devant le Roi, dans l'Af-
" femblée de tous les Omrahs, et marcher
" par les rues tantot à pied tantot en Palcky *.
" Je l'avois auffi vu, et j'avois converfé
" plufieurs fois avec lui, parceque pen-
" dant un an il s'etoit toujours trouvé à
" notre conference devant mon Agah, à
" qui il faifoit la cour, afin qu'il lui fit
" redonner fa penfion, qu' Aurengzebe,
" parvenu à l'Empire, lui avoit otée, pour
" paroitre grand Mufulman. Dans la

* Called by the Englifh *Palankeen*, though the manner in which the French write and pronounce it, is
more correct.—The natives call it *Palke*.

L 4

" vifite

" vifite que je lui rendis à Benares, il me
" fit cent careffes, et me donna même la
" collation dans la Bibliotheque de fon
" Univerfité avec les fix plus fameux Pun-
" dets de la ville. Quand je me vis en fi
" bonne compagnie, je les priai tous, de
" me dire leur fentiment fur l'adoration de
" leurs Idoles ; car je leur difois que je
" m'en allois des Indes extrémement fcan-
" dalifé de ce côté là, et leur reprochois
" que c'étoit une chofe contre toute forte
" de raifon et tout à fait indigne de gens
" favans et Philofophes comme eux :"

" Nous avons veritablement, me dirent
" ils, dans nos temples, quantité de fta-
" tues diverfes, comme celle de Brahma *,
" Mahadeu, Genich, et Gavani †, qui
" font des principaux et des plus parfaits
" *Deutas*, et meme de quantité d'autres
" de moindre perfection, auxquelles nous

---

* This, I prefume, is a miftake ; Bernier probably
meant *Brinha*.

† Probably, Bawany.

" rendons

" rendons beaucoup d'honneur, nous nous
" prosternons devant elles, et leur presen-
" tons des fleurs, du ris, des huiles, de
" senteurs, du safran et autres choses sem-
" blables avec beaucoup de cérémonie :
" néanmoins, nous ne croyons point que
" ces statues soient ou Brahma même, ou
" Eéchen * lui même, et ainsi des autres,
" mais seulement leurs images et represen-
" tations, et nous ne leur rendons ces hon-
" neurs qu'à cause de ce qu'elles repre-
" sentent ; elles sont dans nos *Deuras* †,
" afin qu' il y ait quelque chose devant les
" yeux qui arrête l'esprit ; et quand nous
" prions, ce n'est pas la statue que nous
" prions, mais celui qui est representé par
" la statue : au reste nous reconnoissons
" que c'est Dieu qui est le maitre absolu et
" le seul Tout-puissant."

Mr. Ziegenbalg, one of the first missionaries that was sent by the king of Denmark

---

to Tranquebar *, and who may be named the proteſtant apoſtle of India, having aſked, in writing, from different Brahmans, the reaſon of their not offering worſhip to the Supreme Being, they uniformly re-

---

* Tranquebar was granted to the Danes, by the Rajah of Tanjour, in 1621.—The king of Denmark having applied to M. Francke, profeſſor of theology at Halle, to recommend perſons fit to be ſent as miſſionaries to India, ſelected M. Ziegenbalg and M. Plutchau. They ſailed from Copenhagen the 29th of November 1705, and arrived at Tranquebar the 9th of July 1706. M. Plutchau, after a few years reſidence, returned to Europe, and remained there. M. Ziegenbalg viſited Europe in 1715; came from Denmark to England, embarked there the 4th of March 1716, landed at Madras the 9th of Auguſt of the ſame year, and died at Tranquebar the 23d of February 1719. He tranſlated into the Malabar, or Tamoul language, the whole of the New Teſtament, and at his death had nearly completed a tranſlation of the Old. He wrote a Malabar grammar, that was printed at Halle; and a dictionary, that was printed at Tranquebar in 1712, which then contained 20,000 words, and was afterwards augmented. Vid. Hiſt. du Chriſt. des Indes, par le Croze.

S

plied,

plied, that God was a Being without shape, incomprehensible, of whom no precise idea could be formed; and that the adoration before idols, being ordained by their religion, God would receive, and confider that as adoration offered to himfelf.

Some learned men, or pundits, that he calls *Guanigueuls*, who have written on the *Narghenny worſhip*, or worſhip of the invifible, have no other object of adoration but that Being; and their books treat only of the love of God, and duties of morality. He gives fome literal tranſlations of paſſages from their writings.

" The Being of beings is the only God, " eternal, and every where prefent, who " *comprifes every thing*; there is no God " but thee."

" O Sovereign of all beings, Lord of the " Heavens and the Earth, before whom " ſhall I deplore my wretchednefs, if thou " abandon me * ?"

---

* From a book named Vara-baddu.

" God

" God is, as upon a fea without bounds;
" thofe who wifh to approach him muft
" appeafe the agitation of the waves—they
" muft be of a tranquil and fteady mind,
" retired within themfelves, and their
" thoughts being collected, muft be fixed
" on God only *."

In a letter written to M. Ziegenbalg, by
a Brahman, he fays, " God may be known
" by his laws, and wonderful works. By
" the reafon and underftanding he has
" given to man, and by the creation and
" prefervation of all beings. It is indif-
" penfably the duty of man, to believe in
" God, and love him.—Our law enjoins
" this.—Thofe two principles ought to be
" in his. fpeech, in his mind; they fhould
" guide all his actions, in which being well
" founded, he fhould invoke God, and en-
" deavour in every thing to conform him-
" felf to his will."

---

* From a book named Tchiva-Vackkium.

A Hin-

A Hindoo having been converted to Chriſtianity by the Daniſh miſſionaries, his father wrote to him, " You are yet unac-
" quainted with the myſteries of our re-
" ligion.—We do not worſhip many
" Gods in the extravagant manner you
" imagine.—In all the multitude of images,
" we adore one Divine eſſence only. We
" have amongſt us learned men, to whom
" you ſhould apply, and who will remove
" all your doubts *."

M. de la Croze, in ſpeaking from the authority of M. Ziegenbalg, and another miſſionary, M. J. E. Grundler, ſays, " In
" one of their books, they (the Hindoos)
" expreſs themſelves in the following man-
" ner : The Supreme Being is inviſible, in-
" comprehenſible, immoveable, without
" figure or ſhape. No one has ever ſeen
" him ; time never compriſed him ; his
" eſſence pervades every thing ; all was
" derived from him, &c."

---

* Hiſt. du Chriſt. des Indes, tome ii. liv. 6.

Father

Father Bouchet, superior of the Jesuit missionaries, writes to the bishop of Avranches, from Madura, in the Carnatick.

" The Indians acknowledge one eternal " God, infinitely perfect."

" They say, that the great number of di- " vinities which they worship, are only in- " ferior deities, entirely subject to the will " of the Supreme Being, who is equally " Lord of gods and men *."

Sir William Jones observes, " The " learned Hindoos, as they are instructed " by their own books, in truth acknow- " ledge only one Supreme Being, whom " they call *Brahm*, or the *great one*, in the " neuter gender. They believe his essence " to be infinitely removed from the com- " prehension of any mind but his own, " and they suppose him to manifest his

---

* Lettres Edif. et Cur. 12mo. edit. de Paris, 1781. tome ii.

" power

" power by the operation of his divine
" spirit *."

The vulgar, whose understandings are
only exercised by the usual occupations and
occurrences in their particular spheres of
life; and the feeble, or ignorant, among the
higher ranks of mankind, instead of going
into speculative reflections, naturally fix
their attention on the external object that
is presented to them, which, aided with a
little art, gradually leads them into a super-
stitious veneration of things, to which an
inquiring and thinking mind easily under-
stands that none is due. Nor need we go
to Hindostan for instances of the truth of
this assertion.

If we, therefore, abstract our minds from
the abuses, and inquire into the spirit, of

* Asiatic Researches, vol. i.

the

the Hindoo religion, we fhall find, that it inculcates the belief in one God only, without beginning and without end; nor can any thing be more fublime than their idea of the Supreme Being. I fhall quote fome ftanzas from a hymn to Narrayna, or the Spirit of God, taken, as Sir William Jones informs us, from the writings of their ancient authors.

Spirit of Spirits, who, through ev'ry part
Of fpace expanded, and of endlefs time,
Beyond the reach of lab'ring thought fublime,
Badft uproar into beauteous order ftart;
    Before heav'n was, thou art.

Ere fpheres beneath us roll'd, or fpheres above,
Ere earth in firmamental æther hung,
Thou fat'ft alone, till, through thy myftic love,
Things unexifting to exiftence fprung,
    And grateful defcant fung.

Omnifcient Spirit, whofe all-ruling pow'r
Bids from each fenfe bright emanations beam;
Glows in the rainbow, fparkles in the ftream,
Smiles in the bud, and gliftens in the flow'r
    That crowns each vernal bow'r;

Sighs

Sighs in the gale, and warbles in the throat
Of every bird that hails the bloomy fpring,
Or tells his love in many a liquid note,
Whilft envious artifts touch the rival ftring,
    Till rocks and forefts ring;

Breathes in rich fragrance from the Sandal grove,
Or where the precious mufk-deer playful rove;
In dulcet juice, from cluft'ring fruit diftils,
And burns falubrious in the tafteful clove:
    Soft banks and verd'rous hills
    Thy prefent influence fills;
In air, in floods, in caverns, woods, and plains,
Thy will infpirits all, thy fovereign Maya reigns.

Blue cryftal vault, and elemental fires,
That in th' æthereal fluid blaze and breathe;
Thou, toffing main, whofe fnaky branches wreathe
This penfile orb with intertwifting gyres;
Mountains, whofe lofty fpires,
Prefumptuous, rear their fummits to the fkies,
And blend their em'rald hue with fapphire light;
Smooth meads and lawns, that glow with varying dyes
Of dew-befpangled leaves and bloffoms bright,
Hence! vanifh from my fight
Delufive pictures! unfubftantial fhows!
My foul abforb'd one only Being knows,
Of all perceptions one abundant fource,
Whence ev'ry object, ev'ry moment flows:

Suns hence derive their force,
Hence planets learn their courfe;
But funs and fading worlds I view no more;
God only I perceive; God only I adore.

Brimha, Vifhnou, and Shiva, are undoubtedly only emblems of the power,
the goodnefs, and juftice of the Supreme
Being, and are fometimes called *the three
united in one* *.

In the dialogues between Krifhna and
Arjoon, contained in the Bhagvat Geeta,
Krifhna fays: " I am the creator of all
" things, and all things proceed from me.
" Thofe who are endued with fpiritual
" wifdom know this, and worfhip me."

" I am the foul, which is in the bodies
" of all things. I am the beginning and
" the end. I am time; I am all-grafping

---

* Some of the early Roman Catholic Miffionaries
thought they perceived in the allegory of Brimha,
Vifhnou, and Shivah, a belief in the Holy Trinity.

" death;

" death; and I am the refurrection.   I
" am the feed of all things in nature,
" and there is not any thing animate or
" inanimate without me;

" I am the myftic figure *Oom* *, the
" *Reek*, the *Sam*, and the *Yayoor Veds.*
" I am the witnefs, the comforter, the
" afylum, the friend.   I am generation,
" and diffolution: in me all things are re-
" pofited.

" The whole univerfe was fpread abroad
" by me.

" The foolifh are unacquainted with my
" fupreme and divine nature.   They are

---

* *Oom* is faid to be a myftic word, or emblem, to
fignify the Deity, and to be compofed of Sanfkrit
roots, or letters; the firft of which ftands for Creator;
the fecond, Preferver; and the third Deftroyer.   It
is forbidden to be pronounced, except with extreme
reverence.   An analogy has been found between this
monofyllable and the Egyptian *On*.   WILKINS.

        " of

" of vain hope, of vain endeavours, and
" void of reafon; whilft thofe of true
" wifdom ferve me in their hearts, undi-
" verted by other gods.

" Thofe who worfhip other gods, wor-
" fhip me.   I am in the facrifice, in the
" fpices, in the invocation, in the fire, and
" in the victim."

Arjoon fays in reply : " Thou art the
" prime Creator—Eternal God ! Thou art
" the Supreme ! By thee the univerfe was
" fpread abroad ! Thou art Vayoo, the
" god of the winds; Agnee, the god of
" fire; Varoon, the god of the oceans,
" &c.

" Reverence be unto thee ; again and
" again reverence, O thou, who art all in
" all ! Great is thy power, and great thy
" glory ! Thou art the father of all things ;
                              " where-

" wherefore I bow down, and with my
" body proſtrate on the ground, crave thy
" mercy.   Lord, worthy to be adored!
" bear with me as a father with a ſon; a
" friend with a friend; a lover with the
" beloved."

In ſpeaking of ſerving the Deity, Kriſhna
ſays:

" They who delighting in the welfare
" of all nature, ſerve me in my incor-
" ruptible, ineffable, and inviſible form;
" omnipotent, incomprehenſible, ſtanding
" on high, fixed, and immoveable, with
" ſubdued paſſions, and who are the ſame
" in all things, ſhall come unto me.

" Thoſe whoſe minds are attached to
" my inviſible nature, have the greater
" labour, becauſe an inviſible path is dif-
" ficult to corporeal beings.   Place thy
" heart on me, and penetrate me with thy
" underſtanding, and thou ſhalt hereafter
" enter unto me.   But if thou ſhouldſt
M 3   " be

" be unable at once stedfastly to fix thy
" mind on me, endeavour to find me by
" means of constant practice.

" He, my servant, is dear to me, who
" is free from enmity; merciful, and ex-
" empt from pride and selfishness; who
" is the same in pain and in pleasure;
" patient of wrongs; contented; and
" whose mind is fixed on me alone.

" He is my beloved, of whom man-
" kind is not afraid, and who is not afraid
" of mankind; who is unsolicitous about
" events; to whom praise and blame are
" as one; who is of little speech; who is
" pleased with whatever cometh to pass;
" who has no particular home, and is of
" a steady mind."

In treating of good works, he says:

" Both the desertion and practice of
" works, are the means of happiness.
                                    " But

" But of the two, the practice is to be
" diftinguifhed above the defertion.

" The man, who, performing the duties
" of life, and quitting all intereft in them,
" placeth them upon *Brahm*, the Supreme,
" is not tainted with fin, but remaineth like
" the leaf of the lotus unaffected by the
" waters.

" Let not the motive be in the event:
" be not one of thofe, whofe motive for
" action is in the hope of reward.

" Let not thy life be fpent in inaction:
" perform thy duty, and abandon all
" thoughts of the confequence. The
" miferable and unhappy are fo about the
" event of things; but men, who are en-
" dued with true wifdom, are unmindful
" of the event."

The Hindoos believe, that the foul, after
death, is tried, and, according to the con-

duct

duct of the deceafed, is either rewarded or punifhed. That the fouls of fuch holy men as have arrived to that degree of perfection as entirely to have fubdued their paffions are immediately, and without trial, admitted to eternal happinefs. That the fouls of the wicked, after being confined for a time in *Narekha* *, and punifhed according to their offences, are fent back upon the ftage of life, to animate other bodies, of men or beafts. That even thofe whofe lives have been chequered with good and evil, muft likewife return: And that thefe probations, chaftifements, and tranfmigrations, continue to be repeated, until every vicious inclination be corrected. They fhudder at the idea of eternal punifhment, as incompatible with their notions of the juftice and goodnefs of the Almighty.

---

* Narekha is the name given to the infernal regions, which are fuppofed to be divided into a variety of places adapted to different degrees of punifhment.

It

It is pretended that a few holy men, by ſpecial divine grace, have a knowledge of, or are able to look back on their former ſtates of exiſtence.

It ſeems alſo to be a prevalent opinion with them, that this world, beſides being a ſtate of probation, is likewiſe a ſtate of temporary reward and puniſhment. They ſay, " It cannot be denied that the benefits " which ſome enjoy, are in recompence of " their former virtues ; but ſhould theſe, " in a new life, forget God, and diſobey his " laws, their former conduct will not avail " them, they will be again tried and " judged according to their actions." Nearly the ſame ſentiments were profeſſed by many of the Greek philoſophers.

Notwithſtanding that the Hindoos are ſeparated into the *Viſhnou Bukht* and *Shivah Bukht*, and that a variety of ſects are to be found over the whole penin- ſula, the chief articles of their religion are

are uniform. All believe in *Brahma*, or the Supreme Being; in the immortality of the foul; in a future ftate of rewards and punifhments; in the doctrine of the me-tempfychofis; and all acknowledge the *Veds* as containing the principles of their laws and religion. Nor ought we to wonder at the fchifms that have arifen in fuch a vaft fpace of time, but rather be furprifed, that they have been fo mild in their confequences; efpecially when we reflect on the numbers that arofe amongft ourfelves, and the dreadful effects they produced in a period fo much fhorter.

Their rules of morality are moft benevolent; and hofpitality and charity are not only ftrongly inculcated, but I believe no where more univerfally practifed than amongft the Hindoos.

" Hofpitality is commanded to be exer-
" cifed even towards an enemy, when he
" cometh into thine houfe: the tree doth

" not

" not withdraw its fhade even from the
" wood-cutter.

" Good men extend their charity unto
" the vileft animals. The moon doth not
" withhold her light even from the cot-
" tage of the Chandala *.

" Is this one of us, or is he a ftranger?
" —Such is the reafoning of the ungene-
" rous: but to thofe by whom liberality
" is practifed, the whole world is but as
" one family."

I fhall conclude this chapter with another paffage from the Hectopades, the
valuable truth of which feems, happily,
to be underftood by them.—" There is
" one friend, *Religion*, who attendeth even
" in death, though all other things go to
" decay like the body."

* Outcaft.

SKETCH VII.

Mythology of the Hindoos.

NOtwithstanding what has been said in the foregoing Sketch, it must be owned, that the multitude believe in the existence of inferior deities, which, like the divinities of the Greeks and Romans, are represented under different forms, and with symbols expressive of their different qualities and attributes: all these are however supposed to be inferiour to the triad, *Brimha, Vishnou,* and *Shiva.*

Bawaney*, as the mother of the gods, is held in high veneration, but the other

goddesses

---

* Bawaney, or *Bhavani,* (for I suppose the name to mean the same divinity, and to be only a different

mode

goddesses are always reprefented as the fubordinate powers of their refpective lords.

Brimba is faid to mean, in Sanfkrit, the wifdom of God. He is reprefented with a crown upon his head, and with four hands: in one he holds a fceptre; in another the *Veds* *; in a third a ring, or circle, as an emblem of eternity; and the fourth is empty, being ready to affift and protect his works. Near his image is the *hanfe*, or *flamingo*, on which he is fuppofed to perform his journies.

His goddefs Serafwaty is the patronefs of imagination and invention, of harmony and eloquence. She is ufually reprefented with a mufical inftrument in her hand;

___

mode of fpelling or pronouncing it,) likewife appears in a variety of other characters, as the confort of Maha-Diva, &c.

* See SKETCH V.

and

and is fuppofed to have invented the Deva-
nagry letters, and the Sanfkrit language,
in which the divine laws were conveyed to
mankind.

Sweet grace of Brimha's bed !
Thou, when thy glorious lord
Bade airy nothing breathe and blefs his pow'r,
Sat'ft with illumin'd head,
And, in fublime accord,
Seven fprightly notes to hail th' aufpicious hour,
Led'ft from their fecret bow'r :
They drank the air ; they came
With many a fparkling glance,
And knit the mazy dance,
Like yon bright orbs, that gird the folar flame,
Now parted, now combin'd,
Clear as thy fpeech, and various as thy mind.

Young paffions, at the found,
In fhadowy forms arofe,
O'er hearts, yet uncreated, fure to reign :
Joy, that o'erleaps all bounds,
Grief, that in filence grows,
Hope, that with honey blends the cup of pain,
Pale fear, and ftern difdain,
Grim wrath's avenging band,
Love, nurs'd in dimple fmooth,
That ev'ry pang can footh.

Thee,

Thee, her great parents owns,
All ruling eloquence;
That, like full Ganga, pours her ftream divine,
Alarming ftates and thrones:
To fix the flying fenfe
Of words, thy daughters, by the varied line,
(Stupendous art!) was thine;
Thine, with the pointed reed *,
To give primeval truth
Th' unfading bloom of youth,

And

---

* The pen employed by the Hindoos to write on paper is a fmall reed. To write on leaves, which is the ufual method, they employ a pointed iron inftrument, with which, properly fpeaking, they engrave; the leaves are generally of the palm-tree; they are cut into long regular ftripes, about an inch broad; being of a thick fubftance, and fmooth hard furface, they may be kept for almoft any fpace of time, and the letters have the advantage of not being liable to be effaced or grow fainter. Their books confift of a number of thofe leaves, which by a hole pierced at one end are tied loofely together. After the writing is finifhed, they fometimes rub the leaves with a black powder, which filling up the incifures, renders the letters more confpicuous. In fome parts of India they likewife write on leaves with ink. Engraving on them, feems better adapted to the Indian characters, than it

would

And paint on deathlefs leaves high virtue's meed:
    Fair Science, heav'n-born child,
And playful Fancy on thy bofom fmil'd.

    Who bid the fretted vene
    Start from his deep repofe,
And wakes to melody the quiv'ring frame?
    What youth, with godlike mien,
    O'er his bright fhoulder throws
The verdant gourd that fwells with ftruggling flame
    Nared *, immortal name!
    He, like his potent fire,
    Creative fpreads around
    The mighty world of found,
And calls from fpeaking wood ethereal fire;
    While to th' accordant ftrings
Of boundlefs heav'ns, and heav'nly deeds, he fings.
    But look! the jocund hours
    A lovelier fcene difplay,
Young Hindol fportive in his golden fwing,
    High canopied with flow'rs;
    While Ragnies ever gay
Tofs the light cordage, and in cadence fing
    The fweet return of fpring.

---

would be to thofe in ufe with Europeans, as none of
the former with which I am acquainted, have almoft
any fine ftrokes in them.

    * Nared is the fuppofed fon of Brimha.

In

In the argument to this poem, we are told, that every name, allusion, or epithet, is taken from approved treatises.   It is addressed to Serafwaty, as goddess of harmony: the musical modes are supposed to be demi-gods or genii; and an original *Raga*, or god of the mode, is supposed to preside over each of the six seasons *; each *Raga* is attended by five *Ragnies*, or *nymphs of harmony* †; each has eight sons, or *genii*, of the same divine art; and to each *Raga* and his family is appropriated a distinct sea-

---

* It must be here observed, that there are six seasons in India :

Sĕĕſär, the dewy season.

Hĕĕmät, the cold season.

Väsänt, mild season or spring.

Greeſshmä, hot season.

Värsä, the rainy season.

Särät, breaking, or the breaking up, or end of the rains.   See WILKINS.

† Sir William Jones, in the first volume of the Asiatic Researches, likewise explains the *Ragnies* and *Ragas* to be *paſſions*.

VOL. I.   N   son,

ſon, in which alone his melody can be ſung, or played, at preſcribed hours of the day and night.   The mode of *Dipaca*, or *Cupid the inflamer*, is ſuppoſed to be loſt; and a tradition is current in Hindoſtan, that a muſician who attempted to reſtore it, was conſumed by fire from heaven.

Ah ! where has Dipac veil'd
His flame-encircled head ?
Where flow his lays, too ſweet for mortal ears ?
O loſs how long bewail'd !
Is yellow Cāmōd fled ?
But, earth-born artiſt, hold !
If e'er thy ſoaring lyre
To Dipac's notes aſpire,
Thy ſtrings, thy bow'r, thy breaſt, with rapture bold,
Red light'ning ſhall conſume;
Nor can thy ſweeteſt ſong avert the doom.

The laſt couplet of the poem alludes to the celebrated place of pilgrimage, at the confluence of the *Ganga* and *Yamna*, which the Seraſwaty, another ſacred river, is ſuppoſed to join under ground.

Theſe

Thefe are thy wondrous arts,
    Queen of the flowing fpeech,
Thence Serafwaty nam'd, and Vany bright!
    Oh! joy of mortal hearts,
    Thy myftic wifdom teach,
Expand thy leaves, and, with ethereal light,
    Spangle the veil of night.
    If Lepit pleafe thee more,
    Or Brahmy, awful name!
    Dread Brahmy's aid we claim,
And thirft, Vaedevy, for thy balmy love,
    Drawn from that rubied cave,
Where meek-ey'd pilgrims hail the triple wave.

" The *unarmed Minerva* of the Romans
" apparently correfponds, as patronefs of
" fcience and genius, with Serafwaty, the
" wife of *Brimha* *, and the emblem of his
" principal creative power: both goddeffes
" have given their names to celebrated
" grammatical works; but the *Serefwata*
" of *Sarupacharya*, is far more concife, as

---

* Sir William Jones writes *Brahma*, but I have pre-
fumed to write it *Brimha*, from the opinion that *Brahma* is the Supreme and *Univerfal* Being, and *Brimha*
but an emblem of one of his attributes.

VOL. I.   N 2   " well

" well as more ufeful and agreeable, than
" the Minerva of *Sanctius.* The Minerva
" of Italy invented the flute, and Seraf-
" waty prefides over melody : the protect-
" refs of Athens was even, on the fame ac-
" count, furnamed *Mufice.*"

" Many learned mythologifts, with Gi-
" raldus at their head, confider the *peaceful*
" Minerva as the Ifis of Egypt, from whofe
" temple at Sais a wonderful infcription
" is quoted by Plutarch, which has a re-
" femblance to the four Sanfkrit verfes above
" exhibited, as the text of the Bhagvat.—
" *I am all that hath been, and is, and fhall*
" *be ; and my veil hath no mortal ever re-*
" *moved.* For my part, I have no doubt
" that the Ifwara and Ifi of the Hindoos,
" are the Ofiris and Ifis of the Egyptians,
" though a diftinct effay, in the manner of
" Plutarch, would be requifite, in order to
" demonftrate their identity, &c.*"

---

* See Afiatic Refearches, vol. i. p. 252, 253.

In

In the temples of Vishnou *, this god is worshipped under the form of a human figure, having a circle of heads, and four hands, as emblems of an all-seeing and all-provident being. The figure of the *garoora*, a bird †, on which he is supposed to ride, is frequently to be found immediately in front of his image. Sometimes he is to be seen sitting on a serpent with several heads. They relate many different incarnations of Vishnou. One of his names, in his preserving quality, is Hāry.

" Nearly opposite to Sultan-gunge, a con-
" siderable town in the province of Bahar,
" there stands a rock of granite, forming
" a small island in the midst of the Ganges,
" known by Europeans by the name of
" *the rock of Jehangueery*, which is highly

---

* See Sketc V.

† This sacred bird is a large brown kite, with a white head. The Brahmans, at some of the temples of Vishnou, accustomed birds of that species that may be in the neighbourhood, to come at stated times to be fed, and call them by striking a brass plate.

 " worthy

" worthy the traveller's notice, for a vaft
" number of images carved in relief up-
" on every part of its furface. Amongft
" thefe there is Hāry, of a gigantic fize,
" recumbent upon a coiled ferpent, whofe
" heads, which are numerous, the artift
" has contrived to fpread into a kind of
" canopy over the fleeping god, and from
" each of its mouths iffues a forked tongue,
" feeming to threaten death to any whom
" rafhnefs might prompt to difturb him.
" The whole figure lies almoft detached
" from the block on which it is hewn; is
" finely imagined, and executed with great
" fkill. The Hindoos are taught to believe,
" that at the end of every *kalpa*, or crea-
" tion, all things are abforbed in the deity,
" and that in the interval to another crea-
" tion, he repofeth himfelf on the ferpent
" *Sefha*, duration, and who is alfo called
" *Ananta*, or endlefs *."

---

* Note of Mr. Wilkins to his tranflation of the
Heetopades.

Lechemy

Lechemy is the confort of Vifhnou, and is the goddefs of abundance and profperity. She is likewife named Pedma, Camala, and Sri, *or in the firft cafe Sris.* She may be called Ceres of the Hindoos, and, with a little help from imagination, an affinity may be found in the names. Sir William Jones, in order to ftrengthen this opinion, ingenioufly obferves, that " it " may be contended, that although Lechemy " may be figuratively called the Ceres " of Hindoftan, yet any two or more " idolatrous nations who fubfifted by agri- " culture, might naturally conceive a deity " to prefide over their labours, without " having the leaft intercourfe with each " other; but no reafon appears why two " nations fhould concur in fuppofing " that deity to be a female: one, at leaft, of " them would be more likely to imagine, " that the earth was a goddefs, and that " the God of abundance rendered her fer- " tile. Befides, in very ancient temples

N 4

" near

" near to *Gaya*, we fee images of Lechemy,
" with full breafts, and a *cord* twifted under
" her arm, like a *horn of plenty*, and which
" look very much like the old Grecian and
" Roman figures of Ceres."

Shivah is reprefented under different human forms, and has a variety of names, but is generally called Shivah and Maha-Deva.

Facing the image is that of an ox in a fuppliant pofture; it being fuppofed, that this animal was felected by him as his favourite conveyance.

In his deftroying quality, he appears as a fierce man, with a fnake twined round his neck.

He is alfo called the god of good and evil fortune; and, as fuch, is reprefented with a crefcent in front of his crown.——" May

" he,

" he, on whofe diadem is a crefcent, caufe
" profperity to the people of the earth *."

One of the names of his goddefs is Gow-
ry; who is alfo called Kaly, from *kala*,
time; which, by the Hindoo poets, is always
perfonified, and made the agent of deftruction. But Sir William Jones fays,
that her leading names and characters are,
Parvati, Durga, and *Bhavani.* " As the
" *mountain-born goddefs,* or Parvati, fhe has
" many properties of the Olympian Juno;
" her majeftic deportment, high fpirit,
" and general attributes are the fame; and
" we find her, both on Mount Cailafa and
" at the banquets of the deities, uniformly
" the companion of her hufband."

" She is ufually attended by her fon,
" Carticeya, who rides on a peacock, and,
" in fome drawings, his own robe feems
" to be fpangled with eyes; to which

---

* Heetopades.

" muft

" muft be added, that in fome of her temples,
" a peacock, without a rider, ftands near
" her image.   Though Carticeya, with his
" fix faces and numerous eyes, bears fome
" refemblance to Argus, whom Juno em-
" ployed as her principal wardour, yet as
" he is a deity of the fecond clafs, and the
" commander of celeftial armies, he feems
" clearly to be, the Orus of Egypt, and the
" Mars of Italy."

" The attributes of Durga, or *difficult of*
" *accefs*, are alfo confpicuous, in the fefti-
" val which is called by her name, and in
" this character fhe refembles Minerva; not
" the peaceful inventrefs of the fine and
" ufeful arts, but Pallas, armed with a hel-
" met and fpear: both reprefent heroic
" virtue, or valour united with wifdom;
" both flew demons and giants with their
" own hands; both protected the wife and
" virtuous, who paid them due adoration."
" Indra is the God of *the vifible heavens.*
" His confort is named, Sacki; his celeftial
" city,

" city, Amaravati ; his palace, Vaijayanta ;
" his garden, Nandana ; his chief elephant,
" Airavat ; his charioteer, Matali ; and
" his weapon, Vaira, or the Thunderbolt.
" Though the Eaft is peculiarly under his
" care, his *Olympus* is Meree, or the *north-*
" *pole*, allegorically reprefented as a moun-
" tain of gold and gems *." He is faid to
have a thoufand eyes, and is fometimes
called *the roller of thunder.*

Varoona is the god of the feas and waters,
and is generally reprefented as riding on a
crocodile.

Vayoo is the god of the winds, and rides
on an antelope, with a fabre in his right
hand.

---

* For an inquiry into the affinity between the different Jupiters of the Greeks and Romans, and fome
of the gods of the Hindoos, we refer the reader to the
firft volume of Afiatic Refearches, in the article, *on the
Gods of Greece, Italy, and India,* already mentioned.

Agny

Agny is the god of fire, has four arms, and rides on a ram.

The earth is perfonified by the goddefs Vafoodha, or Vafoo-deva, who, in a verfe of the Heetopades, is called Soerabhy, or the cow of plenty.

Nature is reprefented as a beautiful young woman, named Prakrity.

The Sun is generally called Sour, or *Surya,* " whence the fect who pay him particu- " lar adoration, are called *Souras.* Their " poets and painters defcribe his car as " drawn by feven green horfes *;" though Mr. Fofter informs us, that in the temple of *Bis Eifhuar* at Benaras, there is an ancient piece of fculpture well executed in ftone, reprefenting this god fitting in a car drawn by a horfe with *twelve heads.* His charioteer, and by whom he is preceded, is

---

* Sir William Jones—Afiatic Refearches, vol. i.

Arun,

Arun, or *the dawn*; and among his many
titles, are twelve, " which denote his dif-
" tinct powers in each of the twelve months :
" thofe powers are called Adityas *, or
" fons of Aditi by Cafyapa, the Indian
" Uranus."

" Surya is fuppofed to have defcended fre-
" quently from his car in a human fhape,
" and to have left a race on earth †, equally
" renowned in Indian ftories with the Hi-
" liadai of Greece. It is very fingular, that
" his two fons called Afwinau, or *Afwini-*
" *cumaraw*, in the dual, fhould be confi-
" dered as *twin brothers*, and painted like
" Caftor and Pollux ; but they have each
" the character of Efculapius among the
" gods, and are believed to have been born
" of a nymph, who, in the form of a *mare*,
" was impregnated with fun-beams. I
" fufpect the whole fable of Cafyapa, and

---

* Each of the Adityas has a particular name.
† Sketch III.

" h's

" his progeny, to be aftronomical; and can-
" not but imagine that the Greek name,
" Caffiopeia, has a relation to it.—Another
" great family are called, *the children of the*
" *Moon.*"

" The worfhip of the Solar or Veftal fire,
" may be afcribed, like that of Ofiris and
" Ifis, to the fecond fource of mythology,
" or an enthufiaftick admiration of Nature's
" wonderful powers; and it feems, as far as
" I can yet underftand the *Vedas*, to be the
" principal worfhip recommended in them.
" We have feen that Maha-Deva himfelf
" is perfonated by fire; but fubordinate to
" to him is the god Agny, often called
" Pavaca, or the *purifier*, who anfwers to the
" Vulcan of Egypt, where he was a deity of
" high rank; and his wife Suaha refembles
" the younger Vefta, or Veftia, as the Eolians
" pronounced the Greek word for a
" hearth.—*Bhavani*, or *Venus*, is the confort
" of the fupreme *deftructive* and *generative*

2   " power;

" power; but the Greeks and Romans,
" whofe fyftem is lefs regular than that of
" the Indians, married her to their divine
" artift, whom they named Hephaiftos and
" Vulcan, and who feems to be the Indian
" Vifvacarma, *the forger of arms for the*
" *gods*, and inventor of the Agny-Aftra *."

The Sun is often ftyled king of the Stars
and Planets.

The name of his goddefs is Sangia, who
is fuppofed to be the mother of the river
Jumna.

Chandara, or the moon, is alfo reprefented fitting in a car, but drawn by ante-
lopes, and holding a rabbit in the right
hand.

Ganes is the god of wifdom, or, as he is
fometimes called, of *prudence and policy*. He
is worfhipped before any enterprife.   He is

____

* See SKETCH XII.

repre-

reprefented in a human form, but with an elephant's head, as a fymbol of fagacity; and. is attended by a rat, which is confidered by the Hindoos as an ingenious and provident animal. He has been called the Janus of India. "Few books are begun "without the words, *falutation to Ganes*; "and he is firft invoked by the Brahmans, "who conduct the trial by ordeal, or per- "form the ceremony of the *Homa*, or facri- "fice to fire *."

Vreehafpaty is the god of fcience and learning; and his attendants, the Veedyadharis, or literally, profeffors of fcience, are beautiful young nymphs.

Veek-rama is the god of victory. It is faid to have been the cuftom to facrifice a horfe to him, by letting him loofe in a foreft, and not again employing him.

---

* See Afiatic Refearches, vol. i.—And Voy. aux Indes Orientales, &c. fait par ordre du Roi depuis 1774, jufqu' en 1782, par M. Sonnerat, &c.

Fame

Fame has several names, and is represented as a serpent with a variety of
tongues.

Darma Deva is the god of virtue, and
is sometimes represented by the figure of
a white bull.

Virsavana is the god of riches, and is
generally represented riding on a white
horse. He is likewise called Vitesa, Cuvéra,
and Paulastya. " He is supposed to reside
" in the palace of Alaca, or to be borne
" through the sky in a splendid car, named
" Pushpaca *:" to preside over the northern
regions, " and to be the chief of the *Yak-*
" *shas* and *Rakshas*, two species of good
" and evil genii †."

Dhan-wantary is the god of medicine.
—" When life hath taken its departure,

---

* Sir W. Jones.   † Mr. Wilkins.

" though Dan-wantary were thy phyfician,
" what could he do *?"

Yam Rajah, or Darham Rajah, feems to hold the fame offices with the Hindoos, that Pluto and Minos held with the Greeks. He is judge of the dead, and ruler of the infernal regions. He has a fceptre in his hand, and rides on a buffalo. He was begot by Sour, or the Sun, on a daughter of Bifoo-karma, great architect of the heavenly manfions, and patron of artificers.

Darham Rajah's affiftants are Chiter and Gōpt. The former has the care of reporting the good, the latter, the bad, actions of mankind. And that thefe may be exactly known, two genii attend as fpies on every one of the human race; the fpy of Chiter on the right, and that of Gopt on the left. As foon as any one dies, the

---

* Hectopades.

Jambouts,

Jambouts, or meſſengers of death, convey his ſoul to Darham's tribunal, where his actions are proclaimed, and ſentence immediately paſſed upon him.

Darham Rajah has no power over the ſouls of theſe holy men, whoſe lives have been ſpent in piety and benevolence, unbiaſſed by the hope of reward, or the dread of puniſhment. Theſe are conveyed by genii to the upper regions of happineſs, and are afterwards admitted to *Moukt*, the ſupreme bliſs, or abſorption in the univerſal ſpirit, " though not ſuch as to deſtroy con-" ſciouſneſs in the divine eſſence."

In the Hindoo mythology there are ſeveral accounts of Kriſhen and the nine Gopia, very much reſembling the Apollo and the muſes of the Greeks. Kriſhen is ſuppoſed to be the god Viſhnou in one of his incarnations, and to have come amongſt mankind as the ſon of *Divaci by Vaſudeva*.

He

He was foftered by the fhepherd Ananda, and concealed from the tyrant Canfa, who fought to deftroy him, on account of a prediction that he would die by the hand of a fon of *Vafudeva*. He tended Ananda's flocks on the plains of Matra, a country famous for the beauty of its women, many of whom are fuppofed to have partaken his embraces. " When a boy, he flew the " terrible ferpent Caliya, with many giants " and monfters : at a more advanced age, " he killed his cruel enemy Canfa, and " having taken under his protection king " Judifhter, and the other Pandoos, who " had been oppreffed by the *Kooroos* and " their tyrannical chief, he kindled the war " defcribed in the great Epic Poem, intitled " the Mahabarat, at the profperous con- " clufion of which he returned to his " heavenly feat in Vaicontha, having left " the inftruction comprifed in the Geeta " to his difconfolate friend Arjoon, whofe " grandfon became fovereign of India."

Krifhen

Krishen is likewise called Mohun, *the beloved*; Mænoher, or the heart-catcher, &c.: —He is reprefented as a beautiful young man, fometimes as playing on a mourly, or flute; and to this day he is the favourite divinity of all the Hindoo women.

The god of love has many epithets, defcriptive of his powers, but the ufual one is Kama-diva, or, literally, the god of defire.

In the argument of a hymn to this deity, publifhed at Calcutta, Sir William Jones informs us, " that, according to the " Hindoo mythology, he was the fon of " Maya, or the general attracting power; " that he was married to Retty, or affec- " tion; and that his bofom friend is Vaf- " fant, or the fpring: that he is repre- " fented as a beautiful youth, fometimes " converfing with his mother, or confort,

" in

" in the midft of his gardens and tem-
" ples; fometimes riding by moon-light
" on a parrot, and attended by dancing
" girls, or nymphs, the foremoft of whom
" bears his colours, which are a fifh on a
" red ground: that his favourite place of
" refort is a large tract of country round
" Agra, and principally the plain of Ma-
" tra, where Krifhen alfo and the nine
" Gopia ufually fpend the night with mu-
" fic and dance: that his bow is of fugar-
" cane, or flowers; the ftring, of bees;
" and that his five arrows are each pointed
" with an Indian bloffom, of a heating
" quality."   Many of his names are mentioned in the hymn.

What potent god from Agra's orient bow'rs
Floats through the lucid air; whilft living flow'rs,
With funny twine, the vocal arbours wreathe,
And gales enamour'd heav'nly fragrance breathe?
 Hail, power unknown! for at thy beck
 Vales and groves their bofoms deck,
 And every laughing bloffom dreffes,
 With gems of dew, his mufky treffes.

I feel,

I feel, I feel, thy genial flame divine,
And hallow thee, and kifs thy fhrine.

Know'ft thou not me!——
Yes, fon of Maya, yes, I know
Thy bloomy fhafts and cany bow,
Thy fcaly ftandard, thy myfterious arms,
And all thy pains, and all thy charms.

Almighty Cama! or doth Smara bright,
Or proud Ananga, give thee more delight?
Whate'er thy feat, whate'er thy name,
Seas, earth, and air thy reign proclaim:
All to thee their tribute bring,
And hail thee univerfal king.

Thy confort mild, Affection, ever true,
Graces thy fide, her veft of glowing hue,
And in her train twelve blooming maids advance,
Touch golden ftrings, and knit the mirthful dance.
Thy dreadful implements they bear,
And wave them in the fcented air,
Each with pearls her neck adorning,
Brighter than the tears of morning.
Thy crimfon enfign, which before them flies,
Decks with new ftars the fapphire fkies.

God of the flow'ry fhafts and flow'ry bow,
Delight of all above and all below!
Thy lov'd companion, conftant from his birth
In heav'n clep'd Vaffant, and gay Spring on earth,

Weaves

Weaves thy green robe, and flaunting bow'rs,
And from the clouds draws balmy ſhow'rs,
He with freſh arrows fills thy quiver,
(Sweet the gift, and ſweet the giver,)
And bids the various-warbling throng
Burſt the pent bloſſoms with their ſong.

He bends the luſcious cane, and twiſts the ſtring,
With bees how ſweet ! but ah, how keen their ſting !
He with five flow'rets tips thy ruthleſs darts,
Which through five ſenſes pierce enraptur'd hearts ;
Strong Campa, rich in od'rous gold,
Warm Amer, nurs'd in heav'nly mould,
Dry Nagkezer, in ſilver ſmiling,
Hot Kiticum, our ſenſe beguiling,
And laſt to kindle fierce the ſcorching flame,
Loveſhaft, which gods bright Bela name.
Can men reſiſt thy pow'r, when Kriſhen yields,
Kriſhen, who ſtill in Matra's holy fields
Tunes harps immortal, and to ſtrains divine
Dances by moonlight with the Gopia nine ?

O thou for ages born, yet ever young,
For ages may thy Bramin's lay be ſung ;
And when thy Lory ſpreads his em'rald wings,
To waft thee high above the tower of kings,
Whilſt o'er thy throne the moon's pale light
Pours her ſoft radiance through the night,
And to each floating cloud diſcovers
The haunts of bleſt or joyleſs lovers,

Thy

Thy milder influence to thy bard impart,
'To warm, but not confume, his heart."

When Tanjore was taken by the Englifh, a curious picture was found, reprefenting Kamadiva riding on an elephant,
whofe body was compofed of the figures
of feven young women, entwined in fo
whimfical but ingenious a manner as to
exhibit the fhape of that enormous animal *.

The Eros of the Greeks is found riding
on, and guiding, a lion. The Hindoos
place Kama on an elephant, the ftrongeft
of the brute creation, and perhaps the moft
difficult to be tamed, but afterwards the

---

* Mr. Forfter.

Several pieces of fculpture of the fame figure, in
bas-relief, have been met with in other parts of
Hindoftan.

Sir William Jones mentions *a picture*, of the fame
kind; in which the elephant is compofed of nine
damfels, and the rider is Krifhen.

moft

moſt docile. Here is a degree of analogy ſufficient to excite curioſity, though perhaps not ſufficient to prove that one nation derived the idea from the other. It may have been original with both. They were both poliſhed nations; the power of love is every where felt; and it may naturally have occurred to people of lively and poetical imaginations, to paint the influence of that paſſion, by repreſenting the infant god governing the fierceſt and ſtrongeſt animals.

Nared, the ſon of Brimha, is the Hermes, or Mercury of the Hindoos. " He was a " wiſe legiſlator; great in arts and arms; " an eloquent meſſenger of the gods, either " to one another, or to favoured mortals; " and a muſician of exquiſite ſkill."—" His " actions are a ſubject of a *Poorana*."—" The " law tract, ſuppoſed to have been revealed " by Nared, is at this hour cited by the " Pundits." He was the inventor of the

Vena,

Vena, *or Indian lute*; for a particular description of which we refer the reader to
the Asiatic Researches, vol. i. p. 295.

The idol of Lingam, a deity similar to
the Phallus of the Egyptians, is always to be
found in the interior and most sacred part of
the temples of Shiva.—Sometimes it repre-
sents both the male and female parts of generation, and sometimes only the former. A
lamp is kept constantly burning before it : but
when the Brahmans perform their religious
ceremonies, and make their offerings, which
generally consist of flowers, *seven* lamps are
lighted ; which De la Croze, speaking from
the information of the protestant missionaries, says, exactly resemble the *candelabres*
of the Jews, that are to be seen in the
triumphal arch of Titus.

As the Hindoos depend on their children
for performing those ceremonies to their
manes, which they believe tend to mitigate
punish-

punifhment in a future ftate, they confider the being deprived of them as a fevere misfortune, and the fign of an offended God.

Married women wear a fmall gold Lingam, tied round the neck or arm *; worfhip is paid to Lingam, to obtain fecundity; and among the fables that are told to account for an adoration fo extraordinary, is the following:

" Certain devotees, in a remote time, had acquired great renown and refpect; but the purity of the heart was wanting; nor did their motives and fecret thoughts correfpond with their profeffions and exterior conduct.   They affected poverty,

---

* Sir William Jones obferves, that, " however extra-
" ordinary it may appear to Europeans, it never feems to
" have entered into the heads of the legiflators or people,
" that any thing natural could be offenfively obfcene;
" a fingularity which pervades all their writings and
" converfations, but is no proof of depravity in their
" morals."   Afiatic Refearches, vol. i.

but

but were attached to the things of this life; and the princes and nobles were constantly sending them offerings. They seemed to sequester themselves from the world; they lived retired from the towns; but their dwellings were commodious, and their women numerous and handsome. But nothing can be hid from the gods, and Shivah resolved to expose them to shame. He desired Prakrity * to accompany him; and assumed the appearance of a Pandaram of a graceful form. Prakrity appeared as herself, a damsel of matchless beauty. She went where the devotees were assembled with their disciples, waiting the rising sun to perform their † ablutions and religious ceremonies. As she advanced, the refreshing breeze moving her flowing robe, showed the exquisite shape, which it seemed intended to con-

---

* Nature. See page 188.

† The Hindoos never bathe, nor perform their ablutions, whilst the sun is below the horizon.

ceal.

ceal. With eyes caft down, though fometimes opening with a timid but a tender
look, fhe approached them, and with a
low enchanting voice defired to be admitted
to the facrifice. The devotees gazed on
her with aftonifhment. The fun appeared, but the purifications were forgotten;
the things for the Pooja * lay neglected;
nor was any worfhip thought of but to
her. Quitting the gravity of their manners, they gathered round her, as flies
round the lamp at night, attracted by its
fplendor, but confumed by its flame.
They afked from whence fhe came; whither
fhe was going?—" Be not offended with
" us for our approaching thee; forgive us
" for our importunities. But thou art in-
" capable of anger, thou who art made to
" convey blifs; to thee, who mayeft kill
" by indifference, indignation and refent-
" ment are unknown. But whoever

---

* Pooja, is properly worfhip.

" thou

" thou mayeſt be, whatever motive or ac-
" cident may have brought thee amongſt
" us, admit us into the number of thy
" ſlaves; let us at leaſt have the comfort
" to behold thee."

" Here the words faultered on the lip;
the ſoul ſeemed ready to take its flight;
the vow was forgotten, and the policy of
years was deſtroyed.

" Whilſt the devotees were loſt in their
paſſions, and abſent from their homes,
Shivah entered their village with a muſical
inſtrument in his hand, playing and ſinging like one of thoſe who ſolicit charity.
At the ſound of his voice, the women
quitted their occupations; they ran to ſee
from whom it came. He was beautiful
as Kriſhen on the plains of Matra *. Some

* Kriſhen of Matra, or the Apollo of the Hindoos. See page 195.

dropped

dropped their jewels without turning to look for them; others let fall their garments without perceiving that they difcovered thofe abodes of pleafure, which jealoufy as well as decency has ordered to be concealed. All preffed forward with their offerings; all wifhed to fpeak; all wifhed to be taken totice of; and bringing flowers, and fcattering them before him, faid: " Afkeft thou alms! thou, who art " made to govern hearts! Thou, whofe " countenance is frefh as the morning! " whofe voice is the voice of pleafure; and " thy breath like that of Vaffant * in the " opening rofe! Stay with us, and we will " ferve thee; nor will we trouble thy re- " pofe, but only be jealous how to pleafe " thee."

" The Pandaram continued to play, and fung the loves of Kama †, of Krifhen, and

---

* Vaffant, the fpring.

† Kama, the god of love. See page 197.

3   the

the Gopia ; and fmiling the gentle fmiles of fond defire, he led them to a neighbouring grove, that was confecrated to pleafure and retirement. *Sour* began to gild the weftern mountains, nor were they offended at the retiring day.

" But the defire of repofe fucceeds the wafte of pleafure. Sleep clofed the eyes and lulled the fenfes. In the morning the Pandaram was gone. When they awoke, they looked round with aftonifhment, and again caft their eyes upon the ground. Some directed their looks to thofe who had been formerly remarked for their fcrupulous manners ; but their faces were covered with their veils. After fitting a while in filence, they arofe, and went back to their houfes with flow and troubled fteps. The devotees returned about the fame time from their wanderings after Prakrity. The days that followed were days of embarraffment and fhame. If the women had failed in their

Vol. I.   P   modefty,

modefty, the devotees had broken their
vows. They were vexed at their weaknefs; they were forry for what they had
done; yet the tender figh fometimes broke
forth, and the eye often turned to where
the men firft faw the maid; the women
the Pandaram.

" But the people began to perceive, that
what the devotees now foretold, came not
to pafs. Their difciples, in confequence,
neglected to attend them; and the offerings from the princes and nobles became
lefs frequent than before. They then performed various penances; they fought for
fecret places among the woods, unfre-
quented by man; and having at laft fhut
their eyes from the things of this world,
and retired within themfelves in deep meditation, they difcovered that Shivah was
the author of their misfortunes. Their
underftanding being imperfect; inftead of
bowing the head with humility, they were
inflamed with anger; inftead of contri-

tion

tion for their hypocrify, they fought for vengeance. They performed new facrifices and incantations, which were only allowed to have a certain effect in the end, to fhow the extreme folly of man in not fubmitting to the will of heaven. Their incantations produced a tyger, whofe mouth was like a cavern, and his voice like thunder amongft the mountains. They fent him againft Shivah, who, with Prakrity, was amufing himfelf in the vale. He fmiled at their weaknefs; and killing the tyger at one blow with his club, he covered himfelf with his fkin. Seeing themfelves fruftrated in this attempt, the devotees had recourfe to another, and fent ferpents againft him of the moft deadly kind. But on approaching him they became harmlefs, and he twifted them round his neck. They fent their curfes and imprecations againft him, but they all recoiled upon themfelves. Not yet difheartened by thefe difappointments, they collected all their prayers, their penances, their chari-

ties,

ties, and other good works, the moſt acceptable of all ſacrifices, and demanding in return only vengeance againſt Shivah, they ſent a confuming fire to deſtroy his viril parts. Shivah incenſed at this attempt, turned the fire with indignation againſt the human race; and mankind would ſoon have been deſtroyed, had not Viſhnou, alarmed at the danger, implored him to ſuſpend his wrath. At his intreaties Shivah relented. But it was ordained, that thoſe parts ſhould be worſhipped, which the falſe devotees had impiouſly attempted to deſtroy."

Thoſe who dedicate themſelves to the ſervice of Lingam, ſwear to obſerve inviolable chaſtity. They do not, like the prieſts of Atys, deprive themſelves of the means of breaking their vows; but were it diſcovered, that they had in any way departed from them, the puniſhment is death. They go naked; but being conſidered as

ſanctiſied

sanctified perfons, the women approach them without fcruple, nor is it thought that their modefty fhould be offended by it. Hufbands, whofe wives are barren, folicit them to come to their houfes, or fend their wives to worfhip Lingam at the temples; and it is fuppofed, that the cere-monies on this occafion, if performed with proper zeal, are generally productive of the defired effect.

The figure of Phallus was confecrated to Ofiris, Dionyfus, and Bacchus, who probably were the fame. At the feftivals of Ofiris, it was carried by the women of Egypt, and the figure of Lingam is now borne by thofe of Hindoftan.

The Hindoos, like the Greeks and Romans, have their demi-gods, who drink a beverage called Amrut; and their aërial fpirits, that occupy the fpace in which the globe revolves. Every mountain, wood, and river, has its genii and guardian deity. *Nullus enim locus fine genio eft, qui per anguem plerumque oftenditur.* (SERV. in ÆNEID.) The Greeks afcribed the difeafes to which frail mortality is expofed, to fome angry god, or evil genius.—The Hindoos do the fame.—Pythagoras pretended that the evil genii caufed dreams and difeafes, not only amongft men but animals. (DIOG. LAER. *in Pytha.*)

With a copious mythology, the doctrine of the metempfychofis, and fruitful imaginations, it is not extraordinary that the writings of the Hindoos fhould abound with fables, and tales of metamorphofes, which are read by them with great delight. The relations of the feats of their demi-gods and heroes very much refemble thofe of Bacchus, Hercules, and Thefeus: and the wars of Ram with Ravana, tyrant of the ifland of Ceylon, form the fubject of a beautiful epic poem, called the

Ramayan,

Ramayan, that was written by the famous Hindoo poet Valmie, some thousands of years ago.

They suppose, likewise, that a few souls are peculiarly gifted with the power of quitting their bodies, of mounting into the skies, visiting distant countries, and again returning and resuming them. They call the mystery, or prayer, by which this power is obtained, the *Mandiram*; and in the life of Viramarken it is told, that a certain powerful prince, longing to enjoy this supernatural privilege, went daily, attended only by a confidential page, to a temple situated in a retired and lonely place, where he preferred fervent prayers to the goddess to whom the temple was dedicated, to instruct him in the *Mandiram*. Mortals know not what they ask, and the goodness of the gods is often shewn in not complying with their desires. The goddess, however, at last yielded to his solicitations,

and the myftery was revealed. The flave
had been ordered to remain at a diftance,
but his curiofity being excited by the extreme caution that was obferved, he approached gently to the door of the fanctuary, and learned the fecret, while the high
prieft was inftructing his mafter how the
Mandiram was to be performed. He retired foftly to his ftation. The prince
came out, with the appearance of uncommon joy. He frequently afterwards retired
with the favourite page to the moft un-
frequented parts of a neighbouring foreft, and after recommending to him to fit
and watch over his body, he went and repeated the *Mandiram* in private, when
his foul mounted into the fkies. He
was fo delighted with this new amufement, that he forgot his duty as a ruler;
he was tired of affairs of ftate; he loft
the relifh of his former pleafures; even
his beautiful princefs was neglected; and,
like an early lover with his miftrefs, he

looked

looked impatiently for the hour when he might quit the grandeur of his court, for the fake of foaring, for a moment, above the fpherc of men.—Policy has recommended to princes to be cautious in beftowing their confidence, and not to put it in the power of any one to do them an injury that may not eafily be repaired. One day that the monarch was delighted in his aërial journey, he forgot to come back at the appointed time. The page grew weary with attending, and wifhed to return to the court. He often looked at the body, and again into the air. He thought of a variety of things to divert the tedious hour. The fecret he had learnt at the door of the fanctuary, came into his mind. He who fails in his duty once, generally yields to frefh temptations. Curiofity, that led him from his ftation before the temple, now prompted him to repeat the *Mandiram*. The conflict was but fhort. The myftery was performed. The

foul

foul inftantly quitted the body of the flave. A more graceful form lay before it. The change was preferred. The flave now became the fovereign, and not chufing to have one who had been his mafter for an attendant, he cut off the head of his former body, as being now but a habitation for which he had no longer any ufe. The foul of the prince returned too late. He faw the lifelefs corpfe of his favourite. He guffed what had come to pafs. And after floating, for fome time, over the foreft, and uttering thofe unhappy founds, that are fometimes to be heard in the ftillnefs of the night, he was commanded to enter into the body of a parrot. He flew inftantly to his palace, where, inftead of command-ing, he was caught; and, for the beauty of his plumage, prefented to the princefs, as not unworthy of her regard. He was placed in her apartment; he faw his unfaithful fervant wearing his crown, and enjoying his bed in his ftead ; he heard his late actions examined,

his

his faults criticifed, his foibles turned into ridicule; and when, in the bitternefs of impotent revenge, he repeated all the words of invective he had learnt, they only ferved to amufe the flaves. No one knew the fecret until many ages afterwards, when it was related by a holy hermit *.

Perhaps in no literary refearch we are more liable to be deceived, than in endeavouring to prove the near affinity of one nation to another, by a fimilarity in particular cuftoms and opinions. But notwithftanding my diffidence of argument merely grounded upon fuch a foundation, from what has been even already faid,

---

* The fame ftory, which is likewife mentioned by Father Bouchet, in his letter to M. Huet, Bifhop of Avranches (to be found in *Lettres edif. & cur.* tome xii. p. 170. Edit. de Paris, 1781.) undoubtedly furnifhed the hint to M. de Moncrif, for his beautiful tale of *Les Ames Rivales.* See Oeuvres de Moncrif, tom. ii. p. 17. Edit. Paris, 1768.

there

there appears, fo near a refemblance between the mythology of the Hindoos, and
that of the Egyptians and Greeks, as in-
clines me to believe, that they originate
from one common parent. Sir William
Jones fays, " I am perfuaded that, by
" means of the *Puranas*, we fhall in time
" difcover all the learning of the Egyptians,
" without decyphering their hierogly-
" phics." And I cannot but congratu-
late the public, on an enterprife, from which
we may now reafonably expect much curious, and perhaps ufeful, information.

SKETCH VIII.

THE devotion of the Hindoos confists in going to the temples; in occafion-ally performing certain religious ceremonies at home; in prayers, in faftings, and other penances; in making offerings, both on their own account, and for the fouls of their dead relations; in frequent ablutions, and in charities and pious works.

According to the rules of their religion, they ought to pray thrice a day—in the morning; at noon; and in the evening—*with their faces turned towards the Eaft.* They fhould at the fame time perform their ablutions, and when they have an oppor-tunity, fhould prefer a running ftream to

ftanding

ſtanding waſter. But it is an indiſpenſable duty to waſh themſelves before meals.

The offerings made at the temples generally confiſt of money, fruit, flowers, rice, ſpices, and incenſe. The offering on account of the dead is a cake, called Peenda; which ceremony is performed on the days of the new and full moon.

It has been aſſerted by ſome writers, that the devotion of the Hindoos was formerly ſanguinary, and that even human ſacrifices were offered, as the moſt acceptable to their gods. But the exiſtence of ſuch a practice appears to me extremely queſtionable. As far as I have inveſtigated, the Hindoos ſeem to have been formerly what they are at preſent, mild and humane; and I know not any trace of a cuſtom ſo barbarous, unleſs we conſider in that light thoſe voluntary ſacrifices which ſome enthuſiaſts make of themſelves.

It

It is however true, that in their facred writings mention is made of the Afmavedha Jug *, or facrifice of the horfe; of the facrifice of the white elephant; of the Gomedha Jug, or facrifice of the bull; and even of the Naramedha Jug, or human facrifice.   But it muft be obferved, that the things reprefented as fit to be facrificed, have fo many peculiarities, that we may conclude they were never to be found.   If they have all the requifites that are defcribed, it is faid they will immediately regenerate from their afhes in the fight of the perfons prefent at the facrifice; and that their failing to do fo, denotes the difpleafure of the Supreme Being with thofe who may have caufed the facrifice to be performed. Under that denunciation, and with fo many difficulties, we may fuppofe that fuch facrifices have feldom or never been made; and we are at a lofs to account for their

---

* Jug, is facrifice.

being

being mentioned in their religious writings, unlefs it be to indicate, that nothing in this life is too facred or valuable, to exempt it from being devoted to the fervice of the Almighty.

Yet, notwithftanding what has been here obferved, impartiality, and the attention that is due to whatever may be advanced by one fo well informed in Afiatic hiftory as Sir William Jones, require, that I fhould quote what he has faid on this fubject, and which had not been feen by me till after the firft edition of this work was publifhed.

" The laft of the Greek or Italian divini-
" ties, for whom we find a parallel in the
" Pantheon of India, is the Stygian or
" Taurick Diana, otherwife named Hecate,
" and often confounded with Proferpine;
" and there can be no doubt of her iden-
" tity with Kali, or the wife of Shiva, in

" his

" his character of the Stygian Jove. To
" this black goddefs, with a collar of golden
" fkulls, as we fee her exhibited in all her
" principal temples, *human facrifices* were
" anciently offered, as the Vedas enjoined ;
" but in the *prefent age* *, they are abfo-
" lutely prohibited, as are alfo the facri-
" fices of bulls and horfes : kids are
" ftill offered to her; and to palliate the
" cruelty of the flaughter, which gave
" fuch offence to Budha, the Brahmans
" inculcate a belief, that the poor victims
" rife in the *heaven of Indra* †, where they
" become the muficians of his band. In-
" ftead of the obfolete, and now *illegal*
" facrifices, of a man, a bull, and a horfe,
" called Naramedha, Gomedha, and Af-
" wamedha, the powers of nature are
" thought to be propitiated by the lefs

---

* We prefume that Sir William Jones means the
Kaly Youg.

† See page 186.

" bloody ceremonies at the end of autumn,
" when the festivals of Kali and Lechemi
" are solemnized nearly at the same time.
" Now if it be asked, how the goddess of
" *Death* came to be united with the mild
" patroness of *Abundance*, I must propose
" another question, how came Proserpine
" to be represented in the *European system*
" as the daughter of Ceres?   Perhaps both
" questions may be answered by the pro-
" position of natural philosophers, that
" *the apparent destruction of a substance is*
" *the production of it in a different form.*
" The wild music of Kali's priests at one
" of her festivals brought instantly to my
" recollection, the Scythian measures of
" Diana's adorers in the splendid opera of·
" *Iphigenia in Tauris*, which Gluck ex-
" hibited at Paris, &c."

The sacrifice of the kid to Kali, as above-
mentioned, is probably the same with that
which Father Bouchet calls the *Ekiam*.

                              He

He fays, " The Indians have a facrifice
" called the *Ekiam*, where a fheep is killed;
" the Brahmans, who are forbid to tafte
" meat at other times, are obliged, by the
" law, to partake of the animal that has
" been facrificed;" and, in another place,
" they eat certain parts of the victim, but
" abftain from others; it is only on this
" occafion that they tafte animal food *."

I am informed that a buffalo is likewife
offered to Bawaney, at the feaft of the
Dohra; and thefe are the only inftances
of living facrifices that I am acquainted
with.

The worfhip of the Hindoos may be divided into two forts, the *Narganey Pooja*,
or worfhip of the invifible; and the *Sar-
ganey Pooja*, or the worfhip before idols.

But the followers of the latter are by far the moſt numerous: the former, comparatively ſpeaking, are but few, and in the ſtrict ſenſe of the expreſſion may be termed deiſts. They have either retained the true meaning of their religion from the beginning, or have in later times aboliſhed the fables of the Brahmans, and reſtored it to its original purity. This ſeems to have been a principal object with Veias in his dialogues between Kriſhna and Arjoon; and it appears, that even in his time, above four thouſand years ago, the adoration of the true god was confounded and loſt in an artful and complicated mythology *.

At the hours of public worſhip the people reſort to the temples. They begin their devotions by performing their ablutions at the tank, which is either to be found in

---

* See SKETCH VII. on Mythology.

front

front of the building, or in the great temples, in the centre of the firft court †.·
Leaving their flippers, or fandals, on the border of the tank, they are admitted to a periftile or veftibule, oppofite to the building which contains the idols, where they obferve great reverence; and whilft· the Brahmans perform the ceremonies of the Jug, or the Pooja, the dancing women occafionally dance in the court, finging the praifes of the divinity to the founds of various mufical inftruments.

The Pooja may likewife be performed at home before the houfehold images. Thofe who are to affift at it begin by wafhing

---

† Some of the temples are of an oblong figure, and confift of two or more courts, immediately following each other. Some have only one inclofure, with the chapel where the images are placed, in the center of it; and fome, though few, are like the one at Seringham, having different courts within each other.

them-

themfelves.   They likewife wafh the room
or place deftined for the ceremony; and
then fpread it with a new mat, or with a
carpet that is only ufed for that purpofe.
On this they place *the throne* of the image,
which is generally made of wood richly
carved and gilt, though fometimes of gold
or filver.   The things neceffary for the
Pooja are laid upon the mat; confifting of
a bell of metal; a conch fhell * to blow
on; a cenfer filled with benzoin fugar, and
other articles, which are kept conftantly
burning, by being occafionally renewed.
Flowers feparately and in garlands are fcattered upon the mat.   The idol is put into
a metal bafon, and being wafhed by pouring
water firft on the head, is wiped and placed
on its throne.   Cups, and plates of gold,
filver, or other metals, are fpread before it,
fome filled with rice, others with different

---

* The conch-fhell is held in a fort of veneration by
the Hindoos.

forts of fruits, with dry fweet-meats, and with cow's milk. The worfhippers repeat certain prayers and *Afhlocks*, or verfes in praife of the god whom the idol reprefents.

The Brahman, who performs the ceremony, occafionally rings the bell, and blows the fhell. He gives the *Tiluk*, or mark on the forehead, to the idol, by dipping his right thumb in fome fubftance that has been mixed with water, and prepared for that purpofe. If the mark be a perpendicular one, he begins at the top of the nofe, and advances upwards. But the colour, the fize, and fhape of the *Tiluk* depend on the tribe and feft the worfhippers may be of; fome tribes being marked with vermilion, others with turmerick, and fome with the duft of the whiteft fpecies of fandal wood, &c. A Brahman generally marks all the perfons prefent in the fame manner. The fruit and

Q 4

other

other articles of food that were spread before the idol, are divided amongst them;
and the idol is then carefully wrapped up,
and with the throne and other things used
in the ceremony, kept in a secure place
until another Pooja be performed.

A veneration for the elements, but especially fire and water, seems to have been
common to all the ancient Eastern nations.
The Medes and Persians considered fire
and water as the only true images of the
divinity *; and it is evident, that the
Hindoos, if they do not now worship fire,
hold it in religious respect †. Every day
at sun-rise the priests go to some river, or
to the tanks of their temples, to perform
the Sandivaney, or worship to Brahma the
Supreme. After having washed themselves,
taking water in the right hand, they throw

---

* Herod. i. Clem. Alex. Protrept.
† See page 188. under the article *Sour*.

it

it in the air before and behind them, invoking the Deity, and singing forth thanksgiving and praise.   They then throw some towards the Sun, expressing their gratitude for his having again appeared to dispel the darkness of the night.

Lucian says, that the Indians offered adoration to the Sun, in turning towards the east; and Philostrates observes, that they addressed prayers to him in the morning, to favour the cultivation of the earth; and in the evening, not to abandon them, but return again in the morning.

Father Bouchet says, that " He who " performs the *Ekiam* should, every morn- " ing and evening, put a piece of wood " into the fire, that is employed for that " sacrifice, and take care to prevent it from " being extinguished."

Mr. Wilkins informs us, that the Brahmans are enjoined to light up a fire at certain

times,

times, which muſt be produced by the
friction of two pieces of wood of a particular kind; that with a fire thus procured, their ſacrifices are burnt; the nup-
tial altar flames; and the funeral pile is
kindled.

In the Heetopades it is ſaid: " Fire is
" the ſuperior of the Brahmans; the Brah-
" man is the ſuperior of the tribes; the
" huſband is the ſuperior of women; but
" the ſtranger is the ſuperior of all."

Devotees.

IN every part of Hindoſtan we meet with numbers of devotees, diſtinguiſhed by various names, but not reſtricted to any caſt. They become ſuch from choice, and every Hindoo, except the Chandalah, is at liberty to adopt this mode of life.

Of all the numerous claſſes of devotees, none are ſo much reſpected as the Saniaſſies and Yogeys. They quit their relations, and every concern of this life, and wander about the country without any fixed abode.

It is ſaid, in their ſacred writings, " That " a Saniaſſy, or he who ſhall devote him- " ſelf to a ſolitary religious life, ſhall have

" no

" no other clothing, but what may be ne-
" ceffary to cover his nakednefs; nor any
" other worldly goods but a ftaff in his
" hand, and a pitcher to drink out of.
" That he fhall always meditate on the
" truths contained in the facred writings,
" but never argue on them. That his food
" fhall be confined to rice, and other
" vegetables; and that he fhall eat but once
" a-day, and then fparingly. That he fhall
" look forward with defire to the fepara-
" tion of the foul from the body; be in-
" different about heat, or cold, or hunger,
" or praife, or reproach, or any thing con-
" cerning this life; and that unlefs he
" ftrictly follow thefe rules, and fubdue
" his paffions, he will only be more
" criminal, by embracing a ftate, the du-
" ties of which he could not perform, ne-
" glecting thofe he was born to obferve."

With the precife diftinction between the
Yogey and the Saniaffy, I am unacquainted.
The former in Sanfcrit, fignifies a devout
perfon;

perfon ; the latter, one who has entirely
forfaken the things of this world. It is
faid in the dialogues between Krifhna and
Arjoon,

" Learn, fon of Pandoo, that what they
" call *Sanias*, or a forfaking of the world,
" is the fame with *Yog*, or the practice of
" devotion.

" The man who is happy in his heart,
" at reft in his mind, and enlightened
" within, is a *Yogey*, or one devoted to
" God, of a godly fpirit, and obtaineth
" the immaterial nature of *Brahm* the
" Supreme.

" The man who keepeth the outward
" accidents from entering the mind, and
" his eyes fixed in contemplation between
" his brows ; who maketh the breath pafs
" equally through his noftrils, who hath fet
" his heart upon falvation, and who is
" free from luft, fear, or anger, is for ever
" bleffed in this life."

" He

" He cannot be a *Yogey*, who, in his ac-
" tions, hath not abandoned all views."

" The *Yogey* conſtantly exerciſeth the
" ſpirit in private. He is of a ſubdued
" mind, free from hope. He planteth his
" feat firmly on a ſpot that is neither too
" high nor too low, and ſitteth on the
" ſacred graſs that is called *Koos*, covered
" with a ſkin, or cloth.—There he, whoſe
" buſineſs is the reſtraining of his paſſions,
" ſhould ſit, in the exerciſe of devotion,
" for the purification of his ſoul, keeping
" his head, his neck, and his body ſteady,
" without motion, his eyes fixed on the
" point of his noſe, looking at nothing elſe
" around. The *Yogey* of a ſubdued mind,
" thus employed, in the exerciſe of devo-
" tion, is as a lamp ſtanding in a place
" without wind, which waveth not."

" Supreme happineſs attendeth him
" whoſe mind is thus at peace, whoſe car-
" nal affections and paſſions are ſubdued,
" and who is in God, and free from ſin."

" The

" The man whose mind is endued with
" devotion, beholdeth the supreme soul
" in all things, and all things in the su-
" preme soul."

" The *Yogey* who believeth in unity, and
" worshippeth me present in all things,
" dwelleth in me."

" This divine discipline which is called
" *Yog*, is hard to be attained by him who
" hath not his soul in subjection, but it may
" be acquired by him who taketh pains."

" The *Yogey* is more exalted than the
" *Tapasivees*, those zealots who harass them-
" selves in performing penances."

" He is both a *Yogey* and a *Saniasy* who
" doeth that which he hath to do, inde-
" pendent of the fruit thereof."

" Works are said to be the means by
" which a man may require devotion, so
" rest is called the means for him who hath
" attained devotion."

" When

" When the all-contemplative ~~Saniassy~~ *Saniasy* is
" not engaged with objects of the senses,
" nor in works, then he is called one who
" hath attained devotion."

" The soul of the conquered placid spirit,
" is the same in heat and in cold, in pain
" and in pleasure, in honour and disgrace."

" The man whose mind is replete with
" divine wisdom and learning, who stand-
" eth on the pinnacle, and hath subdued his
" passions, is said to be devout *."

It is not improbable that some of the
passages in the sacred writings which were
enigmatical, being understood literally by
the ignorant, have given rise to those extravagant penances, with which some of
the devotees torture themselves. In one
of the above quotations they seem even to

---

* *Bhagvat Ceeta.* The above quotations, as well
as others, are not taken in the exact order in which
they follow in the work, but are selected from different
parts, as they fuit the subject treated of.

be

be condemned; the *Yogey* being said to be more exalted than the *Tapasivee*, &c. I saw one of the latter, who having made a vow to keep his arms constantly extended over his head, with his hands clasped together, they were become withered and immoveable. Not long ago, one of them finished measuring the distance between Benares and Jaggernaut with his body, by alternately stretching himself upon the ground, and rising; which, if he performed it as faithfully as he pretended, must have taken years to accomplish. Some make vows to keep their arms crossed over their breast for the rest of their days; others to keep their hands for ever shut, and their nails are sometimes seen growing through the back of the hand; some by their own desire, are chained to a particular spot, and others never lie down, but sleep leaning against a tree *.

There

---

* *Philosophos eorum quos Gymnosophistas vocant, ab exortu ad occasum perstare contuentes solem immobilibus*

There are frequent inſtances of devotees and penitents throwing themſelves under the wheels of the chariots * of Shivah or Viſhnou, when the idol is drawn out to celebrate the feaſt of a temple, and being thereby cruſhed to death : and not long ſince we ſaw an account of the aged father of a numerous offspring, who devoted himſelf to the flames, to appeaſe the wrath of a divinity, who, as he imagined, had for ſome time paſt afflicted his family and neighbours with a mortal epidemical diſeaſe.

The *Pandarams*, on the coaſt of Coromandel, are followers of Shivah ; they rub their faces and bodies with the aſhes of burnt cow-dung, and go about the towns and villages ſinging the praiſes of their God.

---

oculis, *ferventibus arenis toto die alternis pedibus inſiſtere.* Plin. lib. vii. cap. 2.—*Gymnoſophiſts* was a name given by the Greeks, on account of their going naked, or probably from their not wearing an upper garment.

* Theſe chariots are more properly great moveable towers, which require many oxen and ſome hundreds of men to draw them.

The *Cary-patry pandarams* are a set of religious perfons, who make a vow never to fpeak; they go to the doors of houfes, and demand charity, by ftriking their hands together. They take nothing but rice, which is given them ready prepared for eating; and, if it be fufficient to fatisfy their hunger, they pafs the reft of the day fitting in the fhade, and fcarcely looking at any object that may come before them.

The *Tadinums* go about begging, and finging the hiftory of the different incarnations of Vifhnou. They beat a kind of tabor; and have fmall brafs bells tied round their ankles, which make a confiderable noife as they walk along.

Thefe devotees are to be met with in every part of Hindoftan; but chiefly in the neighbourhood of great temples, both from religious motives, and in order to receive alms from the pilgrims who refort thither.

Contrary to the practice of the Hindoos in general, many of them wear their hair,

 and,

and, by frequently rubbing it with the oil of the cocoa-nut, it grows to an extraordinary degree of length and thicknefs. Some let it hang loofe on their bodies, extending to the ground; others have it plaited in many treffes, and wound round the head in the form of a great turban.

Moft of the ancient authors who have mentioned India and its inhabitants, feem to have confounded the Devotees, Sectaries, and *Pundits*, or Philofophers, with the Brachmanes, or regular priefthood. They fpeak of *Gymnofophifts*, *Germanes*, *Pramnes*, *Samaniens*, and *Hilobiens*, who are faid to be a clafs of the *Samaniens*, that lived in forefts, and ufed no clothing or nourifhment but what the trees afforded them.

Strabo fays, that the *Samaniens* fet no value on any knowledge but fuch as tended to correct vice, and that they fmiled at thofe who applied themfelves to metaphyfics, aftronomy, and aftrology.—Probably

Strabo

Strabo meant fuch of the *Samaniens* as were *folitaries*, or hermits; for we find that the Samaniens in general were remarked for their learning, and their knowledge in the fciences.

Clement of Alexandria obferves, that there were two claffes of Indian philofophers, the one called *Brachmanes*, the other *Sarmanes*; by which, I am inclined to think, he means the Samaniens. He fays fome of the *Sarmanes* were called *folitaries*, and neither lived in towns nor had any particular dwelling; that they obferved celibacy; and covered their nakednefs with the bark of trees; nourifhed themfelves with their fruit; and drank only water, and that out of the palms of their hands.

Porphyry acquaints us, that the fubftance of the doctrines of the Indians confifted in the neceffity of adoring God with a pure and pious mind; that the *Samaniens*, who fecluded themfelves from the world, infifted on the neceffity of fubduing the paffions, in order to be fit to approach God; and gave that as the reafon for the extraordinary penances they inflicted upon themfelves, *thereby to render the body entirely fubmiffive to the fpirit.*

M. de la Croze fays, that the *Samaniens* are ftill fpoken of with refpect, fo far as regards their learning; but that their doctrines are held in abhorrence by the Brahmans, and that their fect no longer exifts. He fpeaks of feveral of their literary performances. The title of one is Tolkabiam, from its author, who is faid to have been a Hindoo Rajah; we are told, it is very voluminous, and among other things contains the art and rules of Hindoo poetry. M. Ziegenbalg obferves, that to underftand it thoroughly, required long and arduous application.—Another work, called *Diva-garam*, which treats of language and *the choice of words*, is put into the hands of boys who

are

are deſtined to purſue learning, and is held in the higheſt eſteem by their literati, but the ſtyle is ſo exalted as to be entirely above the comprehenſion of the vulgar. .

Calanus *, who burnt himſelf in the prefence of Alexander and his officers, has by ſome been called a Brahman;—but it is evident that he was one of thoſe devotees

---

* We are told that he was ſo named by the Greeks, from his ſaying *Cale*, by way of ſalutation. They likewiſe called him Sphinés, which probably was no more his true name than the other. He was regarded by his countrymen as an apoſtate.—He followed Alexander; at Paſargadus, being attacked with a dyſentery, he ordered a funeral pile to be prepared, and having performed his ablutions, ſacrifices, and prayers, laid himſelf compoſedly down, and was burnt to death. Plut. *Vit. Alex.*

Strabo mentions a perſon who had accompanied ambaſſadors ſent by a prince of India to Auguſtus, that burnt himſelf at Athens; and ſays, the Athenians erected a monument to his memory, with this inſcription, " To *Zarmonæchigas*, Indian of *Bergoſes*, who " voluntarily embraced death, according to the cuſtom " of his country."

who

who travel about the country.—He is faid
to have gone naked; but the Brahmans
neither go naked, nor commit any acts of
extravagance. Their lives are uniform,
indolent but decent; and chiefly occupied
with their rites and ceremonies, they apply
more or lefs to ftudy, according to their
genius and turn of mind.

But notwithftanding this inaccuracy of
ancient authors, in confounding the Brahmans, or regular priefthood, with the devotees and fectaries; if we confider how
limited their intercourfe with India was,
compared to that enjoyed by modern Europeans, and how little we ourfelves knew
of its inhabitants till within thefe few years
paft, we fhall find caufe, inftead of being
fhocked with their errors, to be furprifed at
their inftruction, and perhaps afhamed of
our own fupinenefs. Strabo obferves, that
thofe who had been in India, generally had
feen things but partially, and by the way;
that they had taken their information by

hearfay,

hearſay, which, however, had not prevented their giving accounts as if they had examined with accuracy *.

Some are of opinion, that the extravagant notions of *the illuminated* and *quietiſts*, that have figured among the Chriſtians, and that ſtill exiſt in different parts of Europe, came originally from the devotees of Hindoſtan. D'Herbelot ſays, " The ſect of " the *Illuminés* had its origin in the Eaſt; " it was brought by the Arabs into Spain, " under the name of *Alumbrados*, and has " been renewed in our days by Doctor " Molinos †."

But, beſides the route given to this ſect by D'Herbelot, we find that ſimilar opinions with thoſe of the *Illuminés*, were profeſſed in the eleventh century, by Simeon, ſuperior of a monaſtery of Saint Mamas in Conſtantinople, and were embraced by Pa-

---

* Strabo, 15.

† Bib. Orient. par D' Herbelot, p. 296. fol.

lamas,

lamas, bishop of Salonica. They appeared in the Latin church in the fourteenth century, and broke out and made great progress in the seventeenth, being professed and taught by Molinos, who is considered as the chief of the *Quietists* of the west.

Simeon and others pretended, that, by abstracting themselves from the things of this world, they might, while in a state of such abstraction, and absorbed in the contemplation of God, be received into grace, and partake of the divine essence.—That they then composed a sort of Trinity within themselves, of the body, the soul, and the holy spirit.—While in the practice of contemplation, it was recommended to the disciples, to sit with their chin upon their breast, the eyes fixed on the navel; and they pretended that when they were inspired with the Divine Spirit, they felt it pass through their nostrils, and were affected with peculiarly delightful sensations.— But beside the absurdity of those monstrous

doctrines,

doctrines, which, it might be supposed, would have been sufficient to draw on them the contempt of all reasonable men, it was alleged, that the disciples of Molinos, trusting for their salvation to exercises of *absorption*, were often engaged in scenes of the most licentious debauchery. They were called *Quietists*, from affecting an extraordinary tranquillity of mind; and, however strange it may appear, many of high rank of both sexes, and persons distinguished for their learning, were Quietists. Madame de la Motte Guyon, the friend of the celebrated Fenelon, archbishop of Cambray, openly professed herself to be of the number; nor was he even exempt from suspicion of having adopted some of the opinions of Molinos, though too virtuous and too wise to have credited or practised any of those extravagancies, of which many of the Quietists are accused.

Learning and Philosophy of the Brahmans.

ALL the ancient sacred and profane writings of the Hindoos are written in the Sanskrit language, which is now only known to the *Pundits* *, or men of learning; and is neither spoken nor understood by the rest of the nation. Yet as Sanskrit words are still found in use over the whole peninsula; and as most of the proper names of persons and ancient places are derived from that language, it is not improbable,

---

* Pundit is a Sanskrit word, and an honorary title, signifying doctor or philosopher.

Mr. Wilkins informs us, that Sanskrit is composed from *San*, a preposition, signifying completion, and *skrita*, done or finished.

that

that it was once univerfal, however remote that period may be.

If we compare the Brahmans of the prefent day with the *Brachmanes* * of antiquity, we fhall, in almoft every feature of their character, perceive the ftrongeft refemblance. The difference that may exift between them, may partly have infenfibly taken place in the lapfe of time; but muft chiefly be afcribed to the revolutions that have happened in their government.

The ancient Brahmans, living in an age when the Hindoo empire flourifhed, cultivated fcience with an encouragement of which their oppreffed pofterity are deprived. Befide the ftudy of the facred, moral, and metaphyfical writings of their nation, a principal part of their fcientific purfuits feems to have been directed to

---

* The words are evidently the fame, and derive their origin from Brahma, God.

aftronomy,

aftronomy, natural philofophy, and fome branches of mathematics.

Several ancient authors, in fpeaking of the philofophers of India, fay, that they occupied themfelves with things of a ferious nature; in the contemplation of God and his works; that they fpoke little, and feldom without neceffity, yet never refufed to anfwer thofe who came to them to be inftructed *: that their difcourfe was concife, fententious, often allegorical, and that they fometimes ufed enigmas †.

Nearchus, who commanded Alexander's fleet, faid, that they only refpected truth and virtue ‡.

Strabo informs us, that they cultivated natural philofophy and aftronomy.

They were held in fo high repute for their maxims of morality, and for their

* Strabo, 15. Porphyr. de Abft. 4.
† Diog. Laer. Proœm.
‡ Strabo, ibid.

know-

knowledge in science and philosophy, that, besides Pythagoras, many went from Greece and other more eastern countries, purposely to be instructed by them. Such were, Democrites the Abderian, Pyrrhon, &c. * —— Bardesanes of Babylon, who lived in the time of Alexander Severus, is said to have conversed with the Brachmanes, whom he represented as chiefly occupied in the adoration of God, and the duties of morality †.

Great affinity appears between the manners and practices of the Brahmans and those Gymnosophists of Ethiopia, who settled near the sources of the Nile; and, according to Philostrates, they were descended from the Brahmans. He says, the Gymnosophists of Ethiopia came from India, having been driven from thence for the murder of their king near the Ganges ‡. He makes

---

* Suidas.—Diog. Laert.
† S. Jerom. Porph.
‡ Philost. Vit. Apoll. c. 6.

Pytha-

Pythagoras fay to Thefpefion, in reproaching him for his improper complaifance to the Egyptians, " Admirer as you are of the " philofophy which the Indians invented, " why do you not attribute it to its real pa- " rents, rather than to thofe who are only fo " by adoption? Why afcribe to the Egyptians " a thing as abfurd, as to affert that the " waters of the Nile, mixed with milk, " (which they pretend happened formerly,) " flowed back to their firft fource."—Iarchas, likewife, fays to Apollonius, on afking his opinion concerning the foul: " We think of it what Pythagoras taught " you, and what we taught the Egyp- " tians *."

---

* Philoft. de Vit. Apoll. c. 6. He probably meant the people of the Thebaid, as the opinions of thofe of lower Egypt, with refpect to the Supreme Being, appear in general to have been very different from the tenets of the Hindoos. Some faid, that the foul after death defcended to a fubterraneous place, where it for ever remained; others, that it afcended to the ftars, whence it originally came.

12   Lucian

Lucian obferves, that the fcience of aftronomy came from Ethiopia—perhaps, therefore, from thefe Gymnofophifts who came
originally from Indoftan—And in making
philofophy complain to Jupiter of fome
who had difhonoured her by their conduct,
he fuppofes the Indians to have been the
firft inftructed by her. She fays, " I went
" amongft the Indians, and made them
" come down from their elephants and con-
" verfe with me.—From them I went to
" the Ethiopians, and then came to the
" Egyptians."—Lucian.

But though the Brahmans now may be
inferior to their anceftors, as philofophers
and men of fcience, their *caft* is ftill the only
repofitory of the literature that yet remains:
to them alone is entrufted the education of youth; they are the fole interpre-
ters of the law, and the only expounders
of their religion.

Bernier, in his letter, dated 4th October
1667, gives the following account of their
literary purfuits at that time.

" La ville de Benares, eſt l'école generale,
" et comme l'Athenes de toute la gentilité
" des Indes, où les Brahmens et les Reli-
" gieux, qui ſont ceux qui s'appliquent à
" l'etude, ſe rendent. Ils n'ont point de
" Colleges ni de claſſes ordonnées, comme
" chez nous ; cela me ſemble plus tenir de
" cette façon d'école des anciens, les maitres
" étant diſperſés par la ville dans leur
" maiſons, et principalement dans les Jar-
" dins des Fauxbourgs, ou les gros mar-
" chands les ſouffrent. De ces maitres les
" uns ont quatre diſciples, les autres ſix ou
" ſept, et les plus renommés, douze ou
" quinze tout au plus, qui paſſent les dix et
" les douze années avec eux.   Toute cette
" étude eſt fort froide, parceque la plûpart
" des Indiens ſont d'une humeur lente et
" pareſſeuſe ; la chaleur du pays et leur
" manger y contribuant beaucoup.

" Leur premiere étude eſt ſur le Han-
" ſcrit *, qui eſt une langue tout à fait
" differente de l'Indienne ordinaire et qui

---

* Or Sanſkrit.

" n'eſt

" n'eſt ſue que des Pundits.   Elle s'appelle
" Hanſcrit, qui veut dire langue pure, et
" parcequ'ils tiennent que ce fut dans cette
" langue que Dieu, par le moyen de Brah-
" ma *, leur publia les quatre † Beths qu'ils
" eſtiment livres ſacrés ; ils l'appellent lan-
" gue ſainte et divine: ils pretendent
" même qu'elle eſt auſſi ancienne que Brah-
" ma, dont ils ne comptent l'âge que par
" Lecques, ou centaines de mille ans ; mais
" je voudrois caution de cette étrange an-
" tiquité.   Quoiqu'il en ſoit, on ne ſauroit
" nier, ce me ſemble, qu'elle ne ſoit très an-
" cienne, puiſque leurs livres de religion,
" qui l'eſt ſans doute beaucoup, ne ſont
" écrits que dans cette langue, et que de
" plus, elle a ſes autres de philoſophie, la
" medicine en vers, quelques autres poeſies
" et quantité d'autres livres, dont j'ai vu
" une grande ſale toute pleine dans Benares.

" Apres qu'ils ont apris le Hanſcrit, ce
" qui leur eſt très difficile, parcequ'ils n'ont

---

* He means Brimha.   † Veds.

                              " point.

" point de grammaire qui vaille, ils fe met-
" tent pour l'ordinaire à lire le Purane, qui
" eft comme un interprete et abregé des
" Beths, parceque ces Beths font fort gros,
" du moins fi ce font ceux qu'on me mon-
" tra à Benares : ils font même très rares ;
" jufques-là que mon Agah ne les a jamais
" pu trouver à acheter, quelque diligence
" qu'il ait pu faire ; auffi les tiennent ils fort
" fecrets, de crainte que les Mahometans
" ne mettent la main deffus, et ne les faffent
" bruler, comme ils ont deja fait plufieurs
" fois.

" Entre leurs philofophes il y en a prin-
" cipalement fix fort fameux, qui font fix
" fectes differentes. Les uns s'attachent à
" celle ci, et les autres à celle là, ce qui
" fait de la difference, et caufe même de la
" jaloufie entre les Pundets, ou docteurs ;
" car ils fçavent qu'un tel eft de cette fecte,
" et un tel d'une autre, et chacun d'eux
" pretend que fa doctrine eft bien meilleure
" que celles des autres, et qu'elle eft même
" plus conforme aux Beths.

" Tous

" Tous ces livres parlent des premiers
" principes des chôfes, mais fort differe-
" ment. Les uns tiennent que tout eft
" compofé des petits corps, qui font indivi-
" fibles, non pas à caufe de leur folidité,
" dureté, et refiftance, mais à raifon de
" leur petiteffe, et difent ainfi plufieurs
" chofes enfuite *qui approchent des opinions*
" *de Democrite et d'Epicure.*

" Les autres difent, que tout eft com-
" pofé de matiere et de forme, mais pas un
" d'eux ne s'explique nettement fur la ma-
" tiere, et bien moins encore fur la forme."

" D'autres veulent que tout foit compofé
" des quatre élemens et du néant.

" Il y en a auffi qui veulent que la lu-
" miere et les tenèbres foient les premiers
" principes.

" Il y en a encore qui admettent pour
" principe la privation, ou plutôt les pri-
" vations, qu'ils diftinguent du néant.

S 3

" Il

" Il y en a enfin qui pretendent que
" tout eft compofe d'accidens.

" Touchant ces principes en general,
" ils font tous d'accord qu'ils font éter-
" nels."

The Hindoos, like fome of the ancients,
fuppofe that the foul is an emanation of
the fpirit of God breathed into mortals.
But their manner of expreffing this idea is
more fublime; for, inftead of calling it a
portion of the divine fpirit, they compare
it to the heat and light fent forth from the
fun, which neither leffens nor divides his
own effence: to the fpeech that communi-
cates knowledge, without leffening that
of him who inftructs the ignorant: to
a torch at which other torches are lighted,
without its light being thereby diminifh-
ed, &c.

Some of the philofophers not only believe
that the fouls of mankind are emanations
of

of *the divine spirit*, but that the Sun, the Moon, with the other planets, and all the bodies that are scattered in the infinity of space, are pervaded, and made to exist by this spirit. These opinions are by no means peculiar to the Hindoos, but seem to have been entertained by the Chaldeans, the Persians, and many of the philosophers of Greece and Italy *.

Others giving still greater scope to the imagination, profess the doctrine of *Illusion*. They say nothing really exists in an individual sense, because the universe, and every thing contained in it, is only one, *it is God*, all things being emanations from the first principle. And it is necessary to attend to this doctrine, in order to comprehend many passages in their different authors which refer to it.

---

* Diog. Laert. in Pyth.—Plato in Tim.—Idem in Epin.—Cicero de Nat. Deor.

S 4

Gowtama,

Gowtama *, an ancient author of a metaphyſical work, called *Nayaya-darſana*, makes a diſtinction between what he calls the divine ſoul, and the vital ſoul. The firſt, he ſays, is eternal, immaterial, and indiviſible; reſembling in that reſpect the great Spirit from whence it came: and he thinks it would be monſtrous to imagine, that this eſſence or ſpirit ſhould be affected by the paſſions to which mankind is ſubject. The ſecond, he ſays, is a ſubtle element, which pervades all animated things; and he obſerves, that it would be as abſurd to ſuppoſe that deſire or paſſions of any kind could exiſt in organized matter only, as to ſuppoſe they could exiſt in a piece of mechaniſm that was the work of human ingenuity. Taking it then for

---

* This author is well known to the learned Brahmans. He is mentioned in the Hectopades as a prophet; and the late Colonel Dow tells us, that he depoſited a copy of one of the volumes of his work in the Britiſh Muſeum.

granted,

granted, that mankind partake in a certain degree of the spirit of God, which is not liable to human paſſions; and that organized matter, merely as ſuch, cannot poſſeſs any; the vital ſoul, or pervading element, is that which gives birth to our deſires.

In ſpeaking of man, he mentions, beſides the five external ſenſes of ſeeing, hearing, taſting, ſmelling, and feeling, *one internal ſenſe*; by which we preſume he means intellectual perception.

He ſays, that the external ſenſes convey into the mind diſtinct repreſentations of things; and thereby furniſh it with materials for its internal operations; but that unleſs the mind act in conjunction with the ſenſes, their operation is loſt.— Thus, for inſtance, a perſon in deep contemplation is frequently inſenſible to ſound, nor does he perceive an object that is immediately before his eyes.—That ideas acquired by means of the external ſenſes,

produce

produce new ideas by the internal operation of the mind, and have alfo the power
of exciting fenfations of pain or pleafure.

Reafon, he fays, is the faculty that
enables us to conclude (from what falls
under our immediate obfervation) upon
things at the time not perceptible; as,
when we fee fmoke, we know that it proceeds from fire.—Reafon, he continues,
depends on our ideas, and is in proportion to the nature and extent of them; and
therefore, wherever our ideas are indiftinct,
our reafon muft be imperfect.

By perception, he fays, we have an immediate knowledge of things in a certain
degree, without the aid of reafon; as of a
horfe, a tree, of hard or foft, fweet or
bitter, hot or cold.

He then goes into a difcuffion of infe-
rence; takes notice of true and falfe infe-
rences, and of things that can be demon-
ftrated, and of thofe that cannot.

Memory,

Memory, which he seems to take in a very comprehensive sense, and almost to confound with imagination, may, he says, be employed on things present as to time, but absent as to place; on things past, and on things in *expectation*. He calls memory, the repository of knowledge, from which ideas already acquired, may be occasionally revived and called into action.

In speaking of letters, he says, by that heavenly invention a certain signification being given to figures and characters, the sight of them serves to revive ideas that have been neglected, or were not in action; as well as to convey others we are unacquainted with.—By these, he says, we may increase our knowledge by contemplative experience; by these the actions and discoveries, and learning of men in remote ages, have been transmitted to us: by these the virtues or vices of those of our own times will be transmitted to posterity;

terity; and by thefe we may converfe with thofe we love, however far they may be removed from us.—He then invokes Serafwaty, the goddefs of fcience, by whom they are fuppofed to have been invented.

Treating of duration, he fays, that as we cannot have an idea of its beginning or end, it cannot in its extent be brought within our comprehenfion:—that the duration, which is obvious to our conception, by means of motion and fucceffion, is the fpace between one event and another; as the fpace from the firft appearance of the fun in the morning till he difappears in the evening; and from his difappearing till he appears again; which definite fpace is called time:—that men having invented a mode of meafuring time, or parts of duration, applied it to meafure the revolutions of the planets, from whence proceeded the divifions of time, called years, months, and days, without which invention our knowledge would be confufed, and hiftory unintelligible.

He

He seems to hint at the folly of conjectures about the beginning or duration of the world. But as this, we presume, would not be orthodox with the Brahmans, his sentiments on that subject are so expressed, as to leave great latitude for explanation.

In speaking of the order of nature, as established by the Supreme Being, he observes, that it universally reigns in all his works;—that he therein shows us, that nothing can be produced without a first cause;—and he asks, what is chance, or accident, but a thing of momentary existence, yet always produced by a preceding cause?

In treating of providence and free-will, he supposes, that the Supreme Being, having established the order of nature, leaves her to proceed in her operations, and man to act under the impulse of his desires, restrained and conducted by his reason.— The brutes, he says, act by that impulse only, and employ their natural force or activity simply in the state they were given

to

to them.—But that man, by means of his mental faculties, governs the fierceſt animals, employs the ſtrongeſt and ſwifteſt for his uſe, diſcovers the nature and qualities of every thing the earth produces, and invents mechanic powers far exceeding natural force.—He then goes on to ſhow, that theſe qualities muſt proceed from ſome great and inviſible principle, which God has not imparted to the brute creation, and whoſe exiſtence muſt be ſeparate from the vital ſoul, and independent of organized matter.—He obſerves, that this can no more be doubted, than it can be doubted that the elephant is ſtronger than the deer, or the deer ſwifter than the tortoiſe; but to aſk why it ſhould be ſo, or how it is, would perhaps be impious, and as abſurd as to inquire why God created many of the animals which inhabit the earth, or of the fiſhes that live in the waters.—That we can never be ſufficiently grateful for the portion of that ſpirit he has given us, comparatively limited as it may

be;

be; that having left us unacquainted with the extent of it, we still go on in our researches, in the hope of acquiring farther knowledge, and of making fresh discoveries; and that, by a proper use of it, we may raise our minds above the things of this world, and render ourselves superior to its events.——

Treating of a future state, he says, that such as during their abode on earth have persevered in the practice of piety and virtue, have worshipped God purely from gratitude, love, and admiration, and have done good, without being induced either by the fear of punishment, or the hope of reward, will not stand in need of being purified in *Naraka*, or of again coming into this world to occupy other forms, but will be immediately admitted to celestial happiness.——

This may sufficiently serve as a specimen of the reasoning of this ingenious Hindoo philosopher.

But

But befides Gowtama, many others believe that mankind have two fouls, the one
divine, being an emanation from God;
the other the *fenfitive foul*, which envelopes
the former *, and is placed between it and
the matter of which the body is compofed.

Some, like Pythagoras, fuppofe that the
fouls of animals are endowed with reafon,
and that if they do not always act like
reafonable creatures, it is owing to the
nature and organization of their bodies.
Porphiry, who alleged that not only
animals but plants had fouls, faid, that the
foul did not think or operate in all things
in the fame manner, but according to the
matter with which it was connected.—In
plants it was the *germe*, in animals *intellect*.

In the dialogue already quoted from the
Bhagvat-Geeta, between Krifhna and Ar-
joun, Krifhna fays,

---

* Vid. *Hif. des Dieux Orient.*

" Know

" Know that every thing which is pro-
" duced in nature, refults from the union
" of *Kefhtra* and *Kefhtragna*, matter and
" fpirit.

" Learn that *Prakrity*, nature, and
" *Pouroufh*, are without beginning.

" *Pouroufh*, is that fuperior being who is
" called *Mahefwar*, the great god, the moft
" high fpirit.

" *Karma* is that emanation, from which
" proceedeth the generation of natural
" beings.

" As the all-moving *Akafh* *, from the
" minutenefs of its parts, pafleth every
" where unaffected, even fo the omnipo-
" tent fpirit remaineth in the body unaf-
" fected. And as the fun illumines the
" world, even fo doth the fpirit enlighten
" the body. They who with the eye of

---

* Akafh comes neareft to the *ether* of Profeffor
Euler, being more fubtle than air.

" wifdom perceive the body and the fpirit
" to be diftinct, and that there is a final
" releafe from the animal nature, go to the
" fupreme.

" Thefe bodies, which envelope the fouls
" that inhabit them, are declared to be
" finite beings.   The foul is not a thing of
" which a man may fay, it hath been, or
" is about to be, or is to be hereafter ; for it
" is a thing without birth, conftant and
" eternal, and is not to be deftroyed.   As
" a man throweth away old garments and
" putteth on new, even fo the foul.   The
" weapon divideth it not, the fire burneth
" it not, the wind drieth it not; for it is
" indivifible, inconfumable, incorruptible,
" and is not to be dried away.   There-
" fore believing it to be thus, thou fhouldft
" not grieve.

" It is even a portion of myfelf, that in
" this world is the univerfal fpirit of all
" things.   It draweth together the five

12   " fenfes,

" fenfes, and the *mind*, which is the fixth,
" and *Efwar* *, prefideth over them. The
" foolifh fee it not, but thofe who induf-
" trioufly apply their minds to meditation,
" may perceive this.

" There are three *Goun* arifing from
" *Prakrity*; *Satwa*, truth; *Raja*, paffion;
" and *Tama*, darknefs. The *Satwa Goun*
" is clear, and entwineth the foul with
" fweet and pleafant confequences. The
" love of riches, intemperance, and inordi-
" nate defires, are produced by the pre-
" valency of the *Raja Goun*; and fottifh-
" nefs, idlenefs, gloominefs, and diftrac-
" tion of thought are the tokens of the
" *Tama Goun*. If the mortal frame be
" diffolved whilft the *Satwa* prevaileth, the
" foul proceedeth to the regions of thofe
" beings who are acquainted with the
" Moft High. But if it be diffolved, whilft

* One of the names of the Supreme Being.

T 2

" the

" the *Raja* prevaileth, the foul is born again
" in one of thofe who are attached to the
" fruits of their actions.   And in like
" manner, if it be diffolved while the *Tama*
" is predominant, it is conveyed into fome
" irrational being.

" He who conceiveth *Pouroufh* and
" *Prakrity*, together with the *Goun*, to be
" even as I have defcribed them, is not
" again fubject to mortal birth.

" Thofe who conftantly watch over
" their inordinate defires, are no longer
" confounded in their minds, and afcend
" to that place which endureth for ever.
" Neither the fun, nor the moon, nor the
" fire, enlighteneth that place which is the
" fupreme manfion of my abode.

" He, my fervant, who ferving me
" alone with due attention, has overcome
" the influence of the *Raja* and *Tama Goun*,

" is

" is formed to be abforbed in Brahm the
" Supreme.

" There are who know not what it is to
" proceed in virtue, or recede from vice ;
" nor is veracity, or the practice of good, to
" be found in them. They fay, the world
" is without beginning and without end,
" and without an *Efwar*, and that all
" things are conceived by the junction of
" the fexes. But thefe loft fouls having
" fixed on this vifion, are hypocrites,
" overwhelmed with madnefs and intoxi-
" cation. Becaufe of their folly, they adopt
" falfe doctrines ; they abide by their in-
" conceivable opinions, and determine in
" their minds, that the gratification of the
" fenfual appetites is fupreme happinefs.
" Confounded with various thoughts and
" defigns, and being firmly attached to
" their lufts, they fink at laft into the
" *Narak* of impurity. Wherefore I caft
" down thofe evil fpirits, who thus defpife

T 3

" me ;

" me ; and being doomed to the wombs of
" *Aſoors* * from birth to birth, and not
" finding me, they go into the infernal
" regions."

There is a paſſage in the above quotation
from the Bhagvat Geeta, which ſeems evidently to allude to Atheiſts. " There are
" who know not what it is to proceed in
" virtue, or recede from vice," &c.—It is
ſaid that Atheiſts are ſtill to be found in
Hindoſtan ; and it appears, by a variety of
teſtimonies, that a ſect now exiſts, which
profeſſes doctrines nearly the ſame as thoſe
that were taught by Epicurus.

Father Martin, a jeſuit miſſionary, ſays,
in a letter from Marava, " I forgot to re-
" ply to your Reverence's queſtion, whe-
" ther there are any Atheiſts among theſe

---

* Demons, or evil ſpirits.

" people.

" people. I can only inform you, that
" there is a fect called *Nextagher*, that feems
" to acknowledge no divinity; but it has
" but few partifans, and, generally fpeak-
" ing, all the people of India adore a
" deity *."

De la Croze obferves, " Atheifts are to
" be met with in India, though the num-
" ber is indeed very fmall; and thofe men
" of letters who denied that there were
" any, were mifinformed.—M. Ziegenbalg
" mentions a book named *Karanei Varoubba*
" *Tarein Valamadel*, in which Atheifm is
" openly profeffed. According to the
" fentiments of the Malabars, this work
" *is the production of a Pagan*, and the
" reading of it is ftrictly prohibited †."

---

* Lettres edif. & cur. tome xi. p. 252. Edit. ut
fuprà.

† Hift. du Chrift. des Indes, tom. ii. p. 324. Edit.
ut fuprà.

T 4

De

De la Croze fpeaks of another book found among M. Ziegenbalg's Malabar manufcripts, called *Tchiva-paikkiam*, or the *Felicity of Life*, which he fays is written in verfe, and contains moft excellent maxims of morality. The author, who is known by other poetical works, profeffed no particular worfhip, but maintained that the happinefs of mankind depended on the practice of virtue. He left many profelytes, whofe defcendants, even at this day, have a total indifference about religion : they regard the Chriftian and the Hindoo exactly in the fame manner ; and M. Ziegenbalg obferves, that he had many fruitlefs arguments with them, as they remained firm in their opinions.

It has been afferted by fome writers, that the Hindoos believe in predeftination ; and there are feveral circumftances, as well as paffages in fome of their authors, which feem to give weight to that opinion. But,

upon

upon farther enquiry, it appears, that it is contrary to the principles of their religion; and wherever this belief has obtained, it should be confidered as the private notion of individuals, unwarranted by the eftablifhed doctrines.

The philofopher and Brahman, *Vifhnoa-Sarma*, fays in the *Heetopades* : " It has " been faid, that the determined fate of all " things inevitably happeneth ; and that " whatever is decreed muft come to pafs. " But fuch are the idle fentiments of certain " men. Whilft a man confideth in Pro- " vidence, he fhould not flacken his own " endeavours ; for without labour he can- " not obtain oil from the feed.

" They are weak men who declare fate " to be the fole caufe.

" It is faid, that fate is nothing but the " confequence of deeds committed in a " former ftate of exiftence ; wherefore it " behoveth

" behoveth a man diligently to exert the
" powers he is poſſeſſed of.

" As the potter formeth the lump of clay
" into whatever ſhape he liketh, even ſo
" may a man regulate his own actions.

" Good fortune is the offspring of our
" endeavours, although there be nothing
" ſwecter than eaſe.

" The boy who hath been exerciſed un-
" der the care of his parents, may attain the
" ſtate of an accompliſhed man; but no
" one is a Pundit in the ſtate he came from
" his mother's womb."

Some of their philoſophers inſiſt, that
God created all things perfectly good; that
man, being a free agent, may be guilty of
moral evil; but that this in no way proceeds
from, or affects, the ſyſtem of nature: that
he is to be reſtrained from doing injury to
others,

others, by the rules eftablifhed for the prefervation of order in fociety; and that the
pain and ills which invariably refult from
wicked actions, will alone be a never-fail-
ing punifhment; as the happinefs which a
man receives from doing good, furpaffes
every other human bleffing.

SKETCH XI.

Aftronomy of the Brahmans *.

THE Brahmans are in poffeffion of ancient aftronomical tables, from which
they annually compofe almanacks, and
foretell eclipfes, although they are now,
I believe, unacquainted with the principles
upon which their anceftors conftructed them.
Various predictions, founded upon their

---

* An inquiry into, and a regular account of, the
aftronomy of India, is a work to which I readily acknowledge myfelf unequal: I therefore beg leave to
refer the reader to the works of M. le Gentil and
M. Bailly, and the remarks of Mr. Playfair, contained
in the fecond volume of the Tranfactions of the Royal
Society of Edinburgh.

aftrology,

aftrology, help to fill up thefe almanacks ;
fome days are marked as lucky, and others
as unlucky; and they likewife pretend to
tell fortunes by means of horofcopes.

In their arithmetical calculations they are
remarkably exact.——" Their operations
" are very numerous, ingenious, and diffi-
" cult, but when once learnt, perfectly
" fure. They apply to them from their
" early infancy, and they are fo much ac-
" cuftomed to calculate fums the moft com-
" plicated, that they will do almoft imme-
" diately what Europeans would be long
" in performing. They divide the units
" into a great number of fractions. It is
" a ftudy that feems peculiar to them, and
" which requires much time to learn. The
" moft frequent divifion of the unit is into
" a hundred parts, which is only to be
" learnt confecutively, as the fractions are
" different according to the things that
" are numbered. There are fractions for
" money,

" money, for weights, for meafures, in
" fhort for every thing that may be brought
" to arithmetical operations *."

The Hindoos reckon from the rifing to
the next rifing fun, fixty *nafigey*; each

---

* La Croze.—He obferves, " the fame practice
" undoubtedly exifted among the Romans, which may
" explain fome paffages of ancient authors, as in
" Horace, *Art. Poet.* 325.
 " *Romani pueri longis rationibus affem*
 " *Difcunt in partes centum deducere.*
" It may likewife from hence be underftood what is
" meant by two paffages in Petronius that have hi-
" therto been obfcure. In the firft, a father fays to
" a teacher,
 " *Tibi difcipulus crefcit Cicero meus, jam quatuor partes*
   dicit.
 " In the other, a man fays, boaftingly,
" *Partis centum dico, ad æs, ad pondus, ad nummum.*
" I did not venture to give any examples of the
" calculations of the Indians, though I have many in
" my poffeffion; but I do not in the leaft doubt that
" the arithmetick of the Indians was that of the
" Greeks and Romans."

nafigey

nasigey is divided into sixty *veinary*, and each *veinary* into sixty *taipary*: 2 $\frac{1}{2}$ *nasigey* are equal to one of our hours; 2 $\frac{1}{2}$ *veinary* to one of our minutes; and 2 $\frac{1}{2}$ *taipary*, to one of our seconds: therefore a *nasigey*, or as it may be called *the Hindoo hour*, is equal to 24 of our minutes; and the *veinary*, or *Hindoo minute*, to 24 of our seconds. The astronomical year of the Brahmans, which is said to consist of

N. V. T.
365, 15, 31, 15, answers accordingly to

H. M. Sec.
365, 6, 12, 30.

By Europeans the solar year is now computed at three hundred and sixty-five days five hours forty-eight minutes and fifty-five seconds. It was reckoned by Hipparchus, about 1940 years ago, at three hundred and sixty-five days five hours fifty-five minutes and twelve seconds; and when the astronomical tables

of

of the Brahmans were conftructed, at three hundred and fixty-five days fix hours twelve minutes and thirty feconds. Hence it would appear, that there is a gradual decreafe in the length of the year; and if thefe calculations can be relied upon, we muft conclude, that the earth approaches the fun; that its revolution is thereby fhortened, and that the tables of the Brahmans, or the obfervations that fixed the length of their year, muft have been made near 7300 years ago. The duration given to the year by Hipparchus, was confirmed by Ptolemy, who fucceeded him; and the difference between our calculations and thofe of Hipparchus and Ptolemy, in fome fort eftablifhes the accuracy of thofe of the Brahmans *.

---

* The Brahmans refer to a period 2400 years before the Kaly-youg, or 7292 years ago. See Traité de l'Aftronomie Indienne et Orientale, par M. Bailly. Tranf. of the R. S. at Edinburgh, vol. ii. &c. &c.

Monfieur

Monſieur le Gentil and Monſieur Bailly * have endeavoured to adjuſt the aſtronomical time of the Brahmans to that of the
Europeans.   Monſieur le Gentil ſays:

" C'eſt ce que nous pouvons appeller
" l'année ſyderale des Brames ; mais parce
" que les etoiles avancent ſelon eux, de
" 54 ſecondes tous les ans d'occident en
" orient, on trouve (en ſuppoſant encore
" avec eux le mouvement journalier du
" ſoleil d'un degré) qu'il faut oter 21', 36"
" pour avoir ce que nous appellons l'année
" tropique, ou equinoxiale de 365^d, 5'
" 50", 54"'.

" Cette determination eſt de deux † mi-
" nutes ſeulement plus grande que celle que
" les aſtronomes admettent aujourdhui pour

---

* Traité de l'Aſtronomie Indienne et Orientale, par
Monſieur Bailly, publiſhed in 1787.

† 1. 59.

" la longueur de l'année ; mais elle eſt plus
" petite de $4'\frac{1}{2}$ * ou environ, que celle de
" Hipparque adoptée par Ptolemée, qui
" ſuppoſoit l'année beaucoup trop longue.
" Par conſequent, les anciens Brames con-
" noiſſoient la longueur de l'année ſolaire
" beaucoup mieux que ne l'ont connue
" Hipparque et Ptolemée."

But, according to Monſieur le Gentil's explanation, there would ſtill remain a difference between the time given to the year by the Brahmans, and the modern aſtronomers, of 1 minute and 59 ſeconds ; and ſuch being the caſe, I cannot ſee any good reaſon for admitting this explanation and condemning Hipparchus ; the more eſpecially as his correctneſs with reſpect to the lunar period, is generally allowed.

The Hindoos allot four Yamams, or watches, to the day, and four to the night.

---

* $4'$ 10.

Their

Their week confifts of feven days, to each of which they have given the name of one of the planets, and arranged them exactly in the fame order that has been adopted by Europeans:

Sunday	is Additavaram	{ or the day of the }	Sun
Monday	— Somavaram	—	Moon
Tuefday	— Mangalavaram	—	Mars
Wednefday	— Boutavaram	—	Mercury
Thurfday	— Brahafpativaram	—	Jupiter
Friday	— Soucravaram	—	Venus
Saturday	— Sanyvaram	—	Saturn.

But their planets, like their gods, are frequently called by different names; or are varioufly pronounced in the different dialects, and parts of the empire.

Their year begins on the 11th day of our month of April. They divide it into two equal parts; the one comprifing the time the fun is to the fouth, the other to the north of the equator; and they cele-

brate

brate his return to the north by an annual equinoctial feast.

To adjuft the aftronomical with the civil time, every fourth year is a leap year; in which the time exceeding the 365 days is thrown into one of the 12 months. The number of days in the months is unequal; and fome are of opinion, that in eftablifh-ing the duration of each month, attention has been paid to the time required by the fun to pafs through the different figns of the Zodiac *.

In

---

* Ces mois n'ont pas tous de la même durée, le mois de Juin eft le plus long de tous, et le mois de Decembre le plus court. Cette difference fuppofe que les aftronomes qui les premiers ont travaillé à cette methode Indienne ont connu l'apogée et le perigée du foleil; c'eft à dire qu'ils ont remarqué que le foleil retardoit fon mouvement dans le mois de Juin, et qu'il l'acceleroit pendant le mois de Decembre; qu'il

employoit

In their tables they are put down in the following order :

	Days.	Nas.	Vei.	Tai.
Sitterey, beginning the 11th of April,	30	55	32	0
Vayaſey - beginning in May	31	24	12	0
Any - - in June	31	36	38	0
Ady - in July	31	28	12	0
Avany - - in Auguſt	31	2	10	0
Pivataſſy - in Sept.	30	27	22	0
Arbaſſy - - in Oct.	29	54	7	0
Cartigey - in Nov.	29	30	24	0
Margaii - - in Dec.	29	20	53	●
Tay - in Jan.	29	27	16	0
Maſey - - in Feb.	29	48	24	0
Pangouney - in March	30	20	21	15
	365	15	31	15

In the common time they are reckoned as follows:

---

employoit par conſequent plus de temps à parcourir le ſigne des Gemeaux que celui du Sagittaire. La longueur des autres mois eſt comme le temps que le ſoleil met à parcourir les autres ſignes du zodiaque.

Voy. dans les Mers de l'Inde.

U 3

Bayſatch,

Bayſatch, beginning the 11th of April, has 31 Days
Taith, - - - 31
Aſadeh, - - - 32
Sanvon, - - - 31
Bhadon, - - - 31
Aſan, - - - 31
Catuk, - - - 30
Aghou, - - - 30
Pous, - . - 29
Magh, - - - 29
Phagon, - -' - 30
Tehait, - - - 30

Days 365 *

The lunar month is divided into two parts; that from the new to the full moon, is called *Sood*, or increaſing; and that from the full to the change, *Bole*, or waning. The former is likewiſe ſometimes called *Sookla-pakſha*, or the *light ſide*; and the other, *Kreeſhna-pakſha*, or the *dark ſide*.

---

* In the manner of writing the names of the months for the aſtronomical time, I have followed Monſieur le Gentil, and for the common time Colonel Polier. But it muſt always be remembered, that names are differently pronounced in different parts of India.

5   They

They reckon the duration of the world by four Yougs, but in the length afcribed to them, they are extravagant; and not-withftanding the endeavours of fome ingenious men of fcience, to adjuft their chronology to that of other nations, I do not find, that it has yet been done in a manner by any means fatisfactory.

	YEARS.
The firft, or the Sutty Youg, is faid to have lafted - -	3,200,000
The Tirtah Youg, or fecond age -	2,400,000
The Dwapaar Youg, or third age -	1,600,000
And they pretend the Kaly Youg, or prefent age, will laft - -	400,000

Thefe ages correfpond, in their nature, to the golden, filver, brazen, and iron ages of the Greeks.

They reprefent the four ages under the emblem of a cow.—She denotes virtue, and originally ftood on piety, truth, charity, and humility: but three legs are gone, and fhe is faid to ftand now only on one leg.

U 4

They

They tell us, that in the firſt ages men were greatly ſuperior to the preſent race, both in the length of their lives, and in the powers of their bodies and mental faculties; but that, in conſequence of vice, they gradually declined, and at laſt in this, the *earthen* age, degenerated to what we now ſee them.

At the end of each age, they ſuppoſe that this world is deſtroyed, and that a new creation ſucceeds.

They ſpeak of an author, named *Mun-nou,* or *Menu,* who, they ſay, flouriſhed in the Sutty Youg, or firſt age; of another, Jage Bulk, who is ſuppoſed to have lived in the Tirtah, or ſecond age; and their writings are ſaid to be ſtill extant, and to contain many of the Hindoo laws and cuſtoms. That theſe authors are of great antiquity, we may allow; but the wild date given to their works by the Brahmans, inſtead of increaſing our reſpect for them, makes us ſmile at their credulity: Or, when we con-

ſider

fider their ufual ingenuity, it leads us to imagine, that, like the ancient priefts of Egypt, they have induftrioufly wrapped up the origin of their fpiritual authority in myftery, and thrown it back to a remote period, with a view to fhut out inveftigation, and render inquiry fruitlefs. We fhall therefore abandon thefe fabulous accounts to fuch as may choofe to amufe themfelves with conjectures, and proceed to dates that feem to be fupported by fcience and hiftory.

The beginning of the Kaly Youg, or prefent age, is reckoned from two hours twenty-feven minutes and thirty feconds of the morning of the 16th of February, three thoufand one hundred and two years before the Chriftian æra; but the time for which moft of their aftronomical tables are conftructed, is two days three hours thirty-two minutes and thirty feconds after that, or the 18th February, about fix in the morning *.

---

* See Traité de l'Aftronomie Indienne et Orientale, par Monfieur Bailly, publifhed in 1787.

They

They fay, that there was then a conjunction of the planets; and their tables fhew
that conjunction. Monfieur Bailly obferves, that, by calculation, it appears, that
Jupiter and Mercury were then in the
fame degree of the ecliptic; that Mars was
diftant about eight degrees, and Saturn
feventeen; and it refults from thence, that
at the time of the date given by the Brahmans to the commencement of the Kaly
Youg, they might have feen thofe four
planets fucceffively difengage themfelves
from the rays of the fun; firft Saturn, then
Mars, then Jupiter, and then Mercury.
Thefe four planets, therefore, fhewed themfelves in conjunction, and though Venus
could not have appeared, yet as they only
fpeak in general terms, it was natural
enough to fay, *there was then a conjunction
of the planets.* The account given by the
Brahmans is confirmed by the teftimony of
our European tables, which prove it to be
the refult of a true obfervation: but Monfieur

fieur Bailly is of opinion, that their aftronomical time is dated from an eclipfe of the
moon, which appears then to have happened, and that the conjunction of the
planets is only mentioned by the way. The
caufe of the date given to their civil time he
does not explain, but fuppofes it to be fome
memorable occurrence that we are unacquainted with.   We are by fome told, that
the circumftance which marked that epoch,
was the death of their hero Krifhna, who,
as we have already obferved, was fuppofed
to be the god Vifhnou in one of his incarnations.   Others fay, it was the death of a
famous and beloved fovereign, Rajah Judifhter.   But whichever of the two it may
be, the Hindoos, confidering the event as a
great calamity, diftinguifhed it by beginning a new age, and exprefled their feelings
by its name, the Kaly Youg, *the age of un-
happinefs or misfortune.*

But befides the Kaly Youg, we are acquainted with two other epochs, from which
the Hindoos, in fome parts of India, reckon
their

their civil time. The one commences from the year of the inauguration of a prince named Bickermajit, which happened in the year of the Kaly Youg 3044; and the other from the death of a prince, third in fucceffion from him, called Salbàhàm, who feems to be the Salivaganam of Monfieur le Gentil. The reign of Bickermajit was diftinguifhed by the ftrict adminiftration of juftice, and the encouragement given by him to men of learning. The poet and philofopher Kàldofs was particularly protected by him. By that prince's defire he is faid to have made a collection of the different parts of the Ramayan *, which was difperfed in detached pieces; and he was confidered as the chief of fourteen learned Brahmans, whom Bickermajit invited to his court from different parts of the empire, and diftinguifhed with the appellation *of the fourteen jewels of his crown.*

---

* A celebrated Epic Poem, containing the wars of Rama.

Monfieur

Monſieur Bailly informs us *, that Monſieur de la Loubére, who was ſent ambaſ-
ſador from Louis XIV. to Siam, brought
home from thence in 1687, tables and rules
for the calculation of eclipſes: and that he
likewiſe found in the place, where the charts
belonging to the navy are kept, two manu-
ſcripts containing Hindoo aſtronomical
tables, that were depoſited there by the late
Monſieur de Liſle.

It appears that one ſet of the tables depoſited by M. de Liſle, and here mentioned
by M. Bailly, had been given to him by
father Patouillet, correſpondent of the miſſionaries in India; and that the other ſet
had been ſent to Father Gaubil, by father
Duchamp, who procured them from the
Brahmans at Kriſhnapouram †.

---

* See Traité de l'Aſtronomie Indienne et Orientale,
edition de Paris 1787.

† A town in the Carnatic.—It is written by M.
Bailly, and by Mr. Playfair, in following him,
Chriſnabouram.

The

The tables that were given by father Patouillet, are thought to have come from the neighbourhood of Narſapour *, as they contain a rule for determining the length of the day anſwering to lat. 16°, 16′. N.

Beſides theſe, M. le Gentil brought to Europe, in 1772, other tables and precepts of aſtronomy, that he got from the Brahmans at Tirvalore †.

Here then are four different ſets of tables and precepts of aſtronomy ‡, procured by different perſons, at different times, and from different places, ſome of which are extremely diſtant from the others; yet all, as M. Bailly obſerves, evidently came from the ſame original: all have the ſame motion of the Sun, the ſame duration of the

---

* A town belonging to the Engliſh in the *Northern Circars.*

† A town in the Carnatic in lat. 10°, 44′.

‡ All theſe tables and precepts of aſtronomy are depoſited with the Academy of Sciences at Paris.

year,

year, and all are adapted to the fame meridian, or to meridians at no great diftance, paffing near to Benares.—As for inftance, the tables brought from Siam by M. de la Loubére, fuppofe a reduction of one hour and thirteen minutes of time, or eighteen degrees and fifteen minutes of longitude, weft from the part of Siam to which thofe tables had been adjufted, and which evidently refers to the meridian of Benares.

The tables and precepts above mentioned, contain chiefly, tables and rules for calculating the places of the Sun and Moon, and of the planets; and rules for determining the phafes of eclipfes *.

Monfieur le Gentil mentions, that the method defcribed in the tables which he

---

* See Traité de l'Aftronomie Indienne et Orientale, par M. Bailly.—And Voyage dans les Mers de l'Inde, par M. le Gentil, &c. tome i.

brought

brought home, is called *Fakiam*, or the new, to distinguish it from another established at Benares, called *Siddantam*, or the ancient.—The Pere du Champ also says, that the Hindoos have a method called *Souria Siddantam*, which has served as a rule for the construction of all the tables now existing, and is supposed to be the original and primitive astronomy of the Brahmans: And he observes, that when the Brahmans at Krishnapouram were at a loss in their astronomical calculations, or committed mistakes, they used to say, *this would not have happened if we now understood the Souria Siddantam.*

The epoch of the tables brought from Tirvalore " coincides with the famous " æra of the Kaly-Youg; that is, with the " beginning of the year 3102 before Christ. " When the Brahmans at Tirvalore would " calculate the place of the Sun for a given " time, they begin by reducing into days

" the

" the intervals between that time, and the
" commencement of the Kaly-Youg, mul-
" tiplying the years by 365^d, 6^h, 12$'$,
" 30$''$, and taking away 2^d, 3^h, 32$'$, 30$''$,
" the aftronomical epoch having begun that
" much later than the civil, &c. * "

" The Indian hour has been here reduced
" to the European."

Monfieur Bailly, in treating of thefe
tables, makes the following obfervations:
" Le mouvement Indien dans ce long inter-
" valle, de 4383 ans, ne differt pas d'une
" minute de celui de Caffini ; il eft egale-
" ment conforme a celui des tables de
" Mayer. Ainfi deux peuples, les Indiens
" et les Européens, placés aux deux extré-
" mités du monde, et par des inftitutions
" peut-etre auffi eloignés dans le tems,

" ont obtenu précifement les mêmes ré-
" fultats, quant au mouvement de la lune,
" et une conformité qui ne feroit pas con-
" cevable, fi elle n'etoit pas fondée fur
" l'obfervation, et fur une imitation réci-
" proque de la nature. Remarquons, que
" les quatres tables des Indiens font toutes
" les copies d'une même aftronomie. On
" ne peut nier que les tables de Siam, n'ex-
" iftaffent en 1687, dans le tems que Mon-
" fieur de la Loubère les rapporta de Siam.
" A cette époque les tables de Caffini et de
" Mayer n'exiftoient pas; les Indiens avoient
" deja le mouvement exact que renferment
" ces tables, et nous ne l'avions pas encore.
" Il faut donc convenir que l'exactitude de
" ce mouvement Indien eft le fruit de l'ob-
" fervation. Il eft exact dans cette durée
" de 438 ; ans, parce qu'il a été pris fur le
" ciel même ; et fi l'obfervation en a dé-
" terminé la fin, elle en a marqué egale-
" ment le commencement. C'eft le plus
" long intervalle qui ait été obfervé et dont
" le

" le fouvenir fe foit confervé dans les faftes
" de l'aftronomie. Il a fon origine dans
" l'époque de 3102 ans avant J. C. et il eft
" une preuve démonftrative de la realité de
" cette époque *."

He fays, that the Hindoo tables give an
annual inequality to the moon, fuch as was
difcovered by Tycho Brahé, and which
was unknown to the Alexandrian fchool,
and to the Arabs who fuccceded it.

In the Siamefe tables, " the motions of
" the moon are deduced by certain interca-
" lations, from a period of nineteen years,
" in which fhe makes nearly 235 revolu-
" tions; and it is curious to find at Siam,

---

* See " Le Difcours preliminaire du Traitè de
" l'Aftronomie Indienne et Orientale." Monfieur
Bailly, in a note to pages 36 and 37, fhews that they
could not have received any inftruction from any aftronomer who preceded Caffini, as all, except him, differ
from them very confiderably.

X 2

" the

" the knowledge of that cycle, of which
" the invention was thought to do fo much
" honour to the Athenian aftronomer Meton,
" and which makes fo great a figure in our
" modern kalendars *."

" Cette régle fuppofe donc une periode
" de 19 années, femblable à celle de Méton
" et du nombre d'or; et Dom. Caffini
" ajoute, que la période Indienne eft plus
" exacte que le cycle ancien du nombre
" d'or †."

The Hindoos feem to have known the ufe
of the gnomon at a very remote period; and
at Benares, and other places, many ancient
dia's, of a very curious conftruction and nice
workmanfhip, are yet to be met with.

Their religion commands, that the four
fides of their temples fhould front the car-

---

* Tranf. of the R. S. of Edin. vol. ii. page 144.
† Aftron. Indien. et Oriental. pages 4 and 5.

dinal

dinal points, and they are all fo conftructed.
Monfieur le Gentil obferves:

" Le gnomon fert aux Brames a trouver
" la ligne meridienne, a orienter leur pa-
" godes, et a trouver combien la longueur
" d'un jour quelconque de l'année pris hors
" des equinoxes, excede la durée du jour
" de l'equinoxe, ou eft plus petit que ce
" meme jour.

" L'ufage du gnomon chez eux remonte
" a une tres grande antiquitè, s'ils s'en
" font toujours fervis, pour orienter leurs
" pagodes, comme il y a lieu à le pre-
" fumer *."

" The rule by which the phænomena of
" eclipfes are deduced from the places of
" the fun and moon, have the moft imme-
" diate reference to geometry; and of thefe

----

* Voyage dans les Mers de l'Inde, par M. le Gentil.

                    " rules,

" rules, as found among the Brahmans at
" Tirvalore, M. le Gentil has given a full
" account. ——We have also an account
" by Father du Champ of the method of
" calculation used at Krishnapouram.

" It is a neceffary preparation, in both
" of these, to find the time of the fun's
" continuance above the horizon at the
" place and the day for which the calcu-
" lation of an eclipfe is made; and the
" rule by which the Brahmans refolve this
" problem is extremely fimple and inge-
" nious. At the place for which they cal-
" culate, they obferve the fhadow of a
" gnomon on the day of the equinox, at
" noon, when the fun, as they exprefs it,
" is in the middle of the world. The
" height of the gnomon is divided into
" 720 equal parts, in which parts the
" length of the fhadow is alfo meafured.
" One-third of this meafure is the number
" of minutes by which the day, at the end

" of

" of the firſt month after the equinox, ex-
" ceeds twelve hours ; four-fifths of this
" exceſs, is the increaſe of the day dur-
" ing the ſecond month ; and one-third
" is the increaſe of the day during the
" third month.

" It is plain that this rule involves the
" ſuppoſition, that when the ſun's decli-
" nation is given, the ſame ratio every-
" where exiſts between the arch which
" meaſures the increaſe of the day at any
" place, and the tangent of the latitude ;
" for that tangent is the quotient which
" ariſes from dividing the length of the
" ſhadow by the height of the gnomon.
" Now, this is not ſtrictly true ; for ſuch a
" ratio only ſubſiſts between the chord of
" the arch, and the tangent above men-
" tioned.   The rule is therefore but an ap-
" proximation of the truth, as it neceſſarily
" ſuppoſes the arch in queſtion to be ſo
" ſmall as to coincide nearly with its chord.

X 4   " This

" *This suppofition holds only for places in*
" *low latitudes; and the rule which is founded*
" *on it, though it may fafely be applied in*
" *countries between the tropics, in thofe that*
" *are more remote from the equator, would*
" *lead into errors too confiderable to efcape*
" *obfervation.*

" *As fome of the former rules have ferved*
" *to fix the time, fo does this, in fome mea-*
" *fure, to afcertain the place, of its invention.*
" *It is the fimplification of a general rule,*
" *adapted to the circumftances of the torrid*
" *zone, and fuggefted to the aftronomers of*
" *Hindoftan by their peculiar fituation* *.*"

The Zodiac, or Sodi-Mandalam, is divided into twelve parts or figns, each of
which has its particular name.

" The names and emblems by which
" thofe figns are exprefled, are nearly the

---

* See Tranf. of the R. S. of Edin. vol. ii. p. 170.

" fame

" fame as with us; and as there is nothing

" in the nature of things to have determined

" this coincidence, it muft, like the arrange-

" ment of the days of the week, be the

" refult of fome ancient and unknown

" communication *."

Each fign contains thirty degrees; but the Hindoos alfo divide the twelve figns into twenty-feven parts †, which they call *con-ftellations*, or *places of the moon reckoned in the twelve figns*; every fign is equal to two conftellations and a quarter, each con-ftellation confifts of thirteen degrees twenty minutes, and has its particular name ‡.

" This

---

* See Tranf. of the R. S. of Edin. vol. ii. p. 141.

† Vid. Voyages dans les Mers de l'Inde, par M. le Gentil.—Aftr. Ind. et Orientale, par M. Bailly;—& la Croze, vol. ii. liv. 6.

‡ " Ces 27 conftellations font en effet marquées dans " le ciel par des etoiles. J'emportai avec moi le nom " de chaque conftellation en particulier, et le nombre

" des

" This divifion of the zodiac is extremely
" natural in the infancy of aftronomical
" obfervation, becaufe the moon completes
" her circle among the fixed ftars nearly in
" twenty-feven days, and fo makes an actual
" divifion of that circle into twenty-feven
" equal parts.

" des etoiles qu'il renferme; mais je ne peux pas affurer
" les avoir bien reconnues, parceque beaucoup de ces
" conftellations fortent du cours de notre zodiaque.

" Dans les regles de l'aftronomie Indienne des
" Siamois, que Dominique Caffini nous a données, tome
" viii. des Anciens Mémoires de l'Academie Royale
" des Sciences, p. 234, 235, & 239, il eft dit, que les
" ftations de la lune font les vingtfeptiémes parties du
" zodiaque : les Siamois admettent donc vingt fept
" conftellations, comme les Indiens de la prefqu' ifle
" en deça du Gange ; mais il ne paroît pas que les
" Siamois faffent aucune attention aux étoiles, qui re-
" pondent à ces vingtfeptiémes parties du zodiaque.
" On ne trouve ces vingt-fept conftellations du ze-
" diaque chez aucune autre nation Orientale ; elles
" font donc un ancien monument bien précieux pour
" l'hiftoire de l'aftronomie." Voyage dans les Mers
de l'Inde, par Monfieur le Gentil, de l'Academie des
Sciences, p. 256, 257, &c.

" Thefe

" Thefe *conftellations* are far from in-
" cluding all the ftars in the Zodiac. M.
" le Gentil obferves, that thofe ftars
" feem to have been felected, which are
" beft adapted for marking out, by lines
" drawn between them, the places of the
" moon in her progrefs through the hea-
" vens *."

The preceffion of the equinoxes is
reckoned in their tables at fifty-four feconds in the year : the motion of the ftars
from weft to eaft is found to be at prefent
only about fifty feconds in the year : but
from this motion of fifty-four feconds,
they have evidently formed many of their
calculations. They have a cycle or period
of fixty years, each of which has its particular name ; another of 3,600 years, and
one of 24,000. From the annual motion
given by them to the ftars, of 54 feconds

---

* See Tranf. of the R. S. of Edin. vol. ii. p. 140.

of longitude in the year, 54 minutes of longitude make fixty years, 54 degrees 3,600, and the entire revolution of 360 degrees makes their great period, or *annus magnus*, of 24,000 years, which is often mentioned by them.

Their rules of aftronomy are written in enigmas and in verfe; in verfe, perhaps, to facilitate the retention of them in the memory; and in enigmas, to render them unintelligible to all but thofe who are regularly inftructed, a privilege which is denied both to the Bhyfe and the Soodra.

Monfieur le Gentil obferves, that the Brahmans in general make their calculations with a great degree of quicknefs. He gives an account of a vifit he received foon after his arrival at Pondicherry from a Hindoo, named Nana Moodoo, who, though not a Brahman, had found means, through the fecret protection of perfons in power, to learn fome of the principles of

aftro-

aftronomy. Monfieur le Gentil, to try the extent of his knowledge, gave him fome examples of eclipfes to calculate, and amongft others, one of a total eclipfe of the moon, of the 23d December 1768. Seating himfelf on the floor, he began his work with a parcel of fmall fhells, named Cowries, which he employed to reckon with; and looking occafionally at a book of palm leaves, that contained his rules, he gave the refult of his calculation, with all the different phafes of the eclipfe, in lefs than three quarters of an hour, which, on confronting it with an Ephemeris, Monfieur le Gentil found fufficiently exact, to excite his aftonifhment at the time and manner in which the calculation had been performed. Yet the education of Nana Moodoo, by his own account, muft have been very confined; and Monfieur le Gentil takes notice, that he feemed entirely unacquainted with the

meaning

meaning of many terms, being unable to
explain them.

" Pour la facilité de leurs operations
" aftronomiques, les Brames les ont mifes
" en vers ; chaque terme eft un terme com-
" pofé, et a befoin d'explication pour etre
" compris : par ce moyen les Brames ne font
" entendus de perfonne, ou au moins ne le
" font que de très peu de monde.

" Le Brame, qui avoit enfeigné cet In-
" dien, s'etoit donc refervé le fecret des
" termes, de façon que celuici faifoit
" machinalement fes calculs fans les enten-
" dre ; il trouvoit des refultats, et ne favoit
" point ce qu'ils fignifioient.

" Par exemple ; dans les éclipfes de lune,
" les Brames ont donné à l'argument de
" latitude, le nom de *Patona Chandara,*
" c'eft à dire, la lune offenfée par le
" dragon :

" dragon : Or, le probleme confiste à
" trouver ce Patona Chandara ; l'Indien en
" queftion le trouvoit tres bien, mais il
" n'entendoit point le mot Patona Chan-
" dara, bien loin, qu'il fut, que ce fut la
" diftance de la lune à fon nœud, et ainfi
" du refte *."

In

---

* The *Patona Chandara* accounts for the vulgar
idea among the Hindoos, that the eclipfes are occafioned by a conteft between the fun, or the moon, and
the great ferpent.

Eclipfes are always obferved with fuperftitious ceremonies. The following account is given by Bernier
of thofe he faw on occafion of an eclipfe of the
fun.

" Celle que je vis à Delhi me fembla aufli tres
" remarquable pour les ridicules erreurs et fuperfti-
" tions des Indiens. Au temps qu'elle devoit arriver
" je montai fur la terraffe de ma maifon, qui etoit
" fituée fur le bord de Gemna. De là je vis les deux
" côtés de ce fleuve près d'une lieue de long, couverts
" de gentils, ou idolatres, qui etoient dans l'eau
" jufqu'à la ceinture, regardant attentivement vers le
" ciel, pour fe plonger et fe laver dans le moment
" que

In addition to what has been already
said, tending to shew the superior antiquity
of

" que l'eclipse commenceroit. Les petits garçons et
" les petites filles etoient tout nuds, comme la main.
" Les hommes l'etoient aussi, hormis qu'ils avoient
" une espèce d'écharpe bridée à l'entour des cuisses
" pour les couvrir ; et les femmes mariées et les filles
" qui ne passoient pas six ou sept ans étoient couvertes
" d'une simple drap. Les personnes de condition,
" comme les rajahs, ou princes souverains gentils,
" qui sont ordinairement à la cour au service et à la
" paye du roi, et les serrafs, ou changeurs, banquiers,
" jouaillers, et autres gros marchands, avoient la plû-
" part passé de l'autre côté de l'eau avec toute leur fa-
" mille, et y avoient dressé leurs tentes, et plante dans
" la riviere des Kanates, qui sont une espece de pai-
" avent pour faire leurs ceremonies, et se laver à leur
" aise avec leurs femmes, sans être vus de personne.
" Ces idolatres ne se furent pas plutot apperçus que
" le soleil commençoit de s'eclipser, que j'entendis
" un grand cri qui s'eleva, et que tout d'un coup ils
" se plongerent tous dans l'eau, je ne sais combien de
" fois de suite, se tenant par après debout dans cette
" eau, les yeux et les mains elevées vers le soleil,
" marmotant tous et priant comme on diroit en grande
10   " devotion,

of the aftronomy of the Brahmans, to any
other that Europeans are acquainted with,
I fhall take the liberty to make a few more

" devotion, prenant de temps en temps de l'eau avec
" les mains, la jettant vers le foleil, s'inclinant la
" tête profondement, remuant et tournant les bras et
" les mains, tantôt d'une façon, et tantôt d'une autre,
" et continuant ainfi leurs plongemens, leurs prieres,
" et leurs fingeries jufqu'à la fin de l'eclipfe, quand
" chacun fe retira en jettant des pieces d'argent bien
" avant dans l'eau, et faifant l'aumone aux Brames,
" qui n'avoient pas manqué de fe trouver à cette ce-
" remonie. Je remarquai qu'au fortir de cette ri-
" viere ils prirent tous de vêtemens nouveaux, qui les
" attendoient tout plier fur le fable, et que plufieurs
" des plus devots laifferent là leur anciens habits pour
" les Brames. C'eft ainfi, que de ma terrafle je vis
" celebrer cette grande fête de l'eclipfe, qui fût
" chommée de la même façon dans l'Indus, dans le
" Gange, et dans tous les autres fleuves et talabs, ou
" refervoirs des Indes; mais furtout dans celui de
" Tanaifer, ou il fe trouva plus de cent et cinquante
" mille perfonnes affemblées de tous les côtes des
" Indes, parceque fon eau eft ce jour-la reputée plus
" fainte, et plus meritoire qu'aucune autre."

quotations from the learned and ingenious remarks of Mr. Playfair.

" The moon's mean place, for the beginning of the Kaly-Youg, (that is, for midnight between the 17th and 18th of February, 3102 A. C. at Benares,) calculated from Mayer's tables, on the suppofition that her motion has always been at the fame rate as at the beginning of the prefent century, is 10ˢ 0˚ 51′ 16″—But, according to the fame aftronomer, the moon is fubject to a fmall, but uniform acceleration, fuch that her angular motion, in any one age, is 9″ greater than in the preceding, which, in an interval of 4,801 years, muft have amounted to 5°, 45′, 44″. This muft be added, to give the real mean place of the moon at the aftronomical epoch of the Kaly-Youg, which is therefore 10ˢ, 6°, 37′. —Now, the fame, by the tables of Tirvalore, is 10ˢ, 6°, 0′; the difference is lefs than two-thirds of a degree, which, for fo

remote

remote a period, and confidering the acceleration of the moon's motion, for which no allowance could be made in an Indian calculation, is a degree of accuracy that nothing but actual obfervation could have produced.

" To confirm this conclufion, M. Bailly computes the place of the moon for the fame epoch, by all the tables to which the Indian aftronomers can be fuppofed to have ever had accefs. He begins with the tables of Ptolemy; and if, by help of them, we go back from the æra of Nabonaffar to the epoch of the Kaly-Youg, taking into account the comparative length of the Egyptian and Indian years, together with the difference of meridians between Alexandria and Tirvalore, we fhall find the longitude of the fun, 10°, 21′, 15″ greater, and that of the moon 11°, 52′, 7″ greater, than has juft been found from the Indian tables. At the fame time that this fhews

Y 2

how

how difficult it is to go back, even for a lefs period than that of 3000 years, in an aftronomical computation, it affords a proof altogether demonftrative, *that the Indian aftronomy is not derived from that of Ptolemy.*

" The tables of Ulugh Beig are more accurate than thofe of the Egyptian aftronomer. They were conftructed in a country not far from India, and but a few years earlier than 1491, the epoch of the tables at Krifhnapouram. Their date is July the 4th, at noon, 1437, at Samarcand; and yet they do not agree with the Indian tables, even at the above-mentioned epoch of 1491. But for the year 3102 before Chrift, their difference from them in the place of the fun is 1°, 30', and in that of the moon 6°; which, though much lefs than the former differences, are fufficient to fhow, *that the tables of India are not borrowed from thofe of Tartary.*

" The

" The Arabians employed in their tables the mean motions of Ptolemy; the Perfians did the fame, both in the more ancient tables of Chryfococca, and the later ones of Naffireddin. *It is therefore certain, that the aftronomy of the Brahmans is neither derived from that of the Greeks, the Arabians, the Perfians, or the Tartars.* This appeared fo clear to Caffini, though he had only examined the tables of Siam, and knew nothing of many of the great points which diftinguifh the Indian aftronomy from that of all other nations, that he gives it as his opinion, that thefe tables are neither derived from the Perfian aftronomy of Chryfococca, nor from the Greek aftronomy of Ptolemy; the places they give at their epoch to the apogee of the fun, and of the moon, and their equation for the fun's centre, being very different from both [*]."

---

[*] See Tranf. of the R. S. of Edin. vol. ii. p. 155, &c.

" A for-

" * A formula for computing this in-equality" (in the moon's motion) " has been given by M. de la Place, which though only an approximation, being de-rived from theory, is more accurate than that which Mayer deduced entirely from obfervation; and if it be taken inftead of Mayer's, which laft, on account of its fim-plicity, I have employed in the preceding calculations, it will give a quantity fome-what different, though not fuch as to affect the general refult. It makes the accelera-tion for 4383 years, dated from the be-ginning of the Kaly-Youg, to be greater by 17', 39' than was found from Mayer's rule, and greater, confequently, by 16', 32", than was deduced from the tables of Krifhna-pouram. It is plain, that this coincidence is ftill near enough to leave the argument that is founded on it in poffeffion of all its force, and to afford a ftrong confirma-

---

* See Tranf. of the R. S. of Edin. vol. ii. p. 160.

tion

tion of the accuracy of the theory and the authenticity of the tables.

" That obfervations made in India, when all Europe was barbarous or uninhabited, and inveftigations into the moft fubtle effects of gravitation, made in Europe near five thoufand years afterwards, fhould thus come in mutual fupport of one another, is perhaps the moft ftriking example of the progrefs and viciffitude of fcience, which the hiftory of mankind has yet exhibited.

" This, however, is not the only inftance of the fame kind that will occur, if, from examining the radical places and mean motions in the Indian aftronomy, we proceed to confider fome other of its elements; fuch as, the length of the year, the inequality of the fun's motion, and the obliquity of the ecliptic, and compare them with the conclufions deduced from the

Y 4

theory

theory of gravity by M. de la Grange. To that geometer, phyſical aſtronomy is indebted for one of the moſt beautiful of its diſcoveries, viz.—That all the variations in our ſyſtem are periodical; ſo that though every thing, almoſt without exception, be ſubject to change, it will, after a certain interval, return to the ſame ſtate in which it is at preſent, and leave no room for the introduction of diſorder, or of any irregularity that might conſtantly increaſe. Many of theſe periods, however, are of vaſt duration. A great number of ages, for inſtance, muſt elapſe, before the year be again exactly of the ſame length, or the ſun's equation of the ſame magnitude, as at preſent. An aſtronomy, therefore, which profeſſes to be ſo ancient as the Indian, ought to differ conſiderably from ours in many of its elements. If, indeed, theſe differences are irregular, they are the effects of chance, and muſt be accounted errors; but if they obſerve the

laws,

laws, which theory informs us that the variations in our fyftem do actually obferve, they muft be held as the moft undoubted marks of authenticity *."

Mr. Playfair then goes on to examine this queftion, as M. Bailly has done; and we are perfuaded, if the reader will *impartially* perufe the inveftigations of thefe learned men, he will be fatisfied, that the differences alluded to, are neither the effects of chance, nor to be accounted errors.

After examining the duration given to the year by the Brahmans at the period of the Kaly-Youg, Mr. Playfair proceeds:

" The equation of the fun's centre is an element in the Indian aftronomy, which has a more unequivocal appearance *of belonging to an earlier period than the Kaly-*

---

* See Tranf. of the R. S. of Edin. vol. ii. p. 160, &c.

Youg.

Youg *.   The maximum of *that equation
is fixed, in these tables, at* 2°, 10′, 32″.   It
is at present, according to M. de la Caille,
1°, 55′ ½, that is 15′ less than with the
Brahmans.   Now, M. de la Grange has
shewn, that the sun's equation, together
with the eccentricity of the earth's orbit,
on which it depends, is subject to alternate
diminution and increase, and accordingly
has been diminishing for many ages.   In
the year 3102 before our æra, that equation
was 2°, 6′, 28″ ½; less only by 4′, than in
the tables of the Brahmans.   But if we
suppose the Indian astronomy to be founded
on observations that preceded the Kaly-
Youg, the determination of this equation

---

* M. Bailly, in his remarks on the length of the
years, supposes some of the observations of the Brahmans to have been made during a period often mentioned by them, of 2400 years before the Kaly-Youg,
or, 7,292 years ago.—He takes the medium of that
period 1200 years before the Kaly-Youg, or 6090
years ago.

will

will be found to be still more exact.—
Twelve hundred years before the commencement of that period, or about 4300
before our æra, it appears, by computing
from M. de la Grange's formula, that the
equation of the sun's centre was actually
2°, 8′, 16″; so that if the Indian astronomy be as old as that period, its error
with respect to this equation is but 2′*.

" The obliquity of the ecliptic is another
element in which the Indian astronomy
and the European do not agree, but where
their difference is exactly such as the high
antiquity of the former is found to require.
The Brahmans make the obliquity of the
ecliptic 24°.—Now M. de la Grange's
formula for the variation of the obliquity,
gives 22′, 32″, to be added to its obliquity in 1700, that is, to 23°, 28′, 41″,
in order to have that which took place in

---

* See Transf. of the R. S. of Edin. p. 163.

the

the year 3,102 before our æra. This gives us 23°, 51′, 13″, which is 8′, 47″ ſhort of the determination of the Indian aſtronomers.—But if we ſuppoſe, as in the caſe of the ſun's equation, that the obſervations on which this · determination is founded, were made 1200 years before the Kaly-Youg, we ſhall find that the obliquity of the ecliptic was 23°, 57′, 45″, and that the error of the tables did not much exceed 2′.

" Thus do the meaſures which the Brahmans aſſign to theſe three quantities, the length of the tropical year, the equation of the ſun's centre, and the obliquity of the ecliptic, all agree, in referring the epoch of their determination to the year 3102 before our æra, *or to a period ſtill more ancient*. This coincidence in three elements, altogether independent of one another, cannot be the effect of chance. The difference, with reſpect to each of them, be-

tween

tween their aftronomy and ours, might fingly perhaps be afcribed to inaccuracy; but that three errors, which chance had introduced, fhould be all of fuch magnitude as to fuit exactly the fame hypothefis concerning their origin, is hardly to be conceived.—Yet there is no other alternative, but to admit this very improbable fuppofition, or to acknowledge, that the Indian aftronomy is as ancient as one or other of the periods abovementioned *.

. " In feeking for the caufe of the fecular equations, which modern aftronomers have found it neceffary to apply to the mean motion of Jupiter and Saturn, M. de la Place has difcovered, that there are inequalities belonging to both thefe planets,

---

* See Tranf. of the R. S. of Edin. p. 164.

In fuppofing the time neceffary for the progrefs of knowledge in that fcience, we muft look to periods much beyond thofe.

arifing

arifing from their mutual action on one another, which have long periods, one of them no lefs than 877 years; fo that the mean motion muft appear different, if it be determined from obfervations made in different parts of thofe periods. " Now I " find," fays he, " by my theory, that at " the Indian epoch of 3102 years before " Chrift, the apparent and annual mean " motion of Saturn was 12°, 13', 14", and " the Indian tables make it 12°, 13', 13".

" In like manner, I find, that the annual " and apparent mean motion of Jupiter at " that epoch, was 30°, 20', 42", precifely as " in the Indian aftronomy."

" Thus have we enumerated no lefs than nine aftronomical elements *, to which the tables

---

* " The inequality or the preceffion of the equinoxes; the acceleration of the moon ; the length of the folar year ;

tables of India affign fuch values as do by no means belong to them in thefe later ages, but fuch as the theory of gravity proves to have belonged to them three thou-fand years before the Chriftian æra.   At that time, therefore, or *in the ages pre-ceding it*, the obfervations muft have been made from which thefe elements were de-duced.   For it is abundantly evident, that the Brahmans of later times, however willing they might be to adapt their tables to fo remarkable an epoch as the Kaly-Youg, could never think of doing fo, by fubftituting, inftead of quantities which they had obferved, others which they had no reafon to believe had ever exifted.   The elements in queftion are precifely what thefe aftronomers muft have fuppofed in-

---

year; the equation of the fun's centre; the obliquity of the ecliptic; the place of Jupiter's aphelion; the equation of Saturn's centre; and the inequalities in the mean motion of both thefe planets."

variable,

variable, and of which, had they fuppofed them to change, they had no rules to go by for afcertaining the variations; fince to the difcovery of thefe rules is required, not only all the perfection to which aftronomy is at this day brought in Europe, but all that which the fciences of motion and of extenfion have likewife attained. It is no lefs clear that thefe coincidences are not the work of accident; for it will fcarcely be fuppofed that chance has adjufted the errors of the Indian aftronomy with fuch fingular felicity, that obfervers, who could not difcover the true ftate of the heavens, at the age in which they lived, have fuc-ceeded in defcribing one which took place feveral thoufand years before they were born *.

" The preceding calculations muft have required the affiftance of many fubfidiary

----

* See Tranf. of the R. S. of Edin. vol. ii. p. 169.

tables,

tables, of which no trace has yet been found in India.   Besides many other geometrical propositions, some of them also involve the ratio which the diameter of a circle was supposed to bear to its circumference, but which we would find it impossible to discover from them exactly, on account of the small quantities that may have been neglected in their calculations.   Fortunately, we can arrive at this knowledge, which is very material when the progress of geometry is to be estimated, from a passage in the *Ayin Akbaree**, where we are told that the Hindoos suppose the diameter of a circle to be to its circumference as 1250 to 3927; and where the author, *who believed it to be perfectly exact*, expresses his astonishment, that, among so simple a people, there should be found a truth, which among the wisest and most learned nations had been sought for in vain.

* See SKETCH III. p. 94.

" The proportion of 1250 to 3927, is indeed a near approach to the quadrature of the circle; it differs little from that of Metius, 113 to 355, and is the fame with one equally well known, that of 1 to 3.1416. When found in the fimpleft and moft elementary way, it requires a polygon of 768 fides to be infcribed in a circle; an operation which cannot be arithmetically performed without the knowledge of fome very curious properties of that curve, and at leaft nine extractions of the fquare root, each as far as ten places of decimals. All this muft have been accomplifhed in India; for, it is to be obferved, that the above-mentioned proportion cannot have been received from the mathematicians of the weft. The Greeks left nothing on this fubject more accurate than the theorem of Archimedes; and the Arabian mathematicians feem not to have attempted any nearer approximation. The geometry of modern Europe can much lefs be re-

garded

garded as the fource of this knowledge.
Metius and Vieta were the firft who, in
the quadrature of the circle, furpaffed the
accuracy of Archimedes; they flourifhed
at the very time when the Inftitutes of
Akbar were collected in India *."—But the
fcience of the Brahmans was then buried
under the ruins of the Hindoo empire.

" On the grounds which have now been
explained the following general conclufions appear to be eftablifhed.

" 1ft, The obfervations on which the
aftronomy of India is founded, were made
more than three thoufand years before the
Chriftian æra; and, in particular, the places
of the fun and moon, at the beginning of
the Kaly-Youg, were determined by actual
obfervation.

---

* See Tranf. of the R. S. of Edin. vol. ii. p. 185.

" This

" This follows from the exact agreement of the radical places in the tables of Tirvalore, with thofe deduced for the fame epoch from the tables of De la Caille and Mayer, and efpecially in the cafe of the moon when regard is had to her acceleration. It follows, too, from the pofition of the fixed ftars in refpect of the equinox, as reprefented in the Indian zodiac; from the length of the folar year; and laftly, from the pofition and form of the orbits of Jupiter and Saturn, as well as their mean motions; in all of which, the tables of the Brahmans, compared with ours, give the quantity of the change that has taken place, juft equal to that which the action of the planets on one another may be fhewn to have produced, in the fpace of forty-eight centuries, reckoned back from the beginning of the prefent.

" Two other of the elements of this aftronomy, the equation of the fun's centre, and

and the obliquity of the ecliptic, when compared with thofe of the prefent time, feem to point to a period ftill more remote, and to fix the origin of this aftronomy 1,000 or 1200 years earlier; that is, 4,300 years before the Chriftian æra *: and the time neceffary to have brought the arts of calculating and obferving to fuch perfection as they muft have attained at the beginning

---

* That they point to a period more remote than the beginning of the Kaly-Youg, I imagine that the impartial reader will not now deny; but I hope to be excufed in faying, that I cannot fee any reafon for dating the *origin* of the Indian aftronomy, at 1000 or 1200 years before that. Perhaps it fhould rather be faid, that the Brahmans, 4,300 years before the Chriftian æra, muft have been in poffeffion of fuch or fuch parts of their aftronomy. It is poffible that materials may yet be found, to enable Mr. Playfair to carry his refearches ftill farther back into antiquity; but probably never to afcertain the origin of a fcience, which was not delivered ready written, like a book of laws, but begun by looking at the heavens, and improved, through the courfe, perhaps, of many ages, by obfervation and experience.

of

of the Kaly-Youg, comes in fupport of the fame conclufion.

" Of fuch high antiquity, therefore, muft we fuppofe the origin of this aftronomy, unlefs we can believe, that all the coincidences which have been enumerated are but the effects of chance ; or, what indeed were ftill more wonderful, that, fome years ago, there had arifen a Newton among the Brahmans, to difcover that univerfal principle, which connects, not only the moft diftant regions of fpace, but the moft remote periods of duration ; and a De la Grange, to trace, through the immenfity of both, its moft fubtle and complicated operations.

" 2dly, Though the aftronomy that is now in the hands of the Brahmans is fo ancient in its origin, yet it contains many rules and tables that are of later conftruction.

" The

" The firft operation for computing the moon's place from the tables of Tirvalore, requires that 1,600,984 days fhould be fubtracted from the time that has elapfed fince the beginning of the Kaly-Youg, which brings down the date of the rule to the year 1282 of our æra. At this time, too, the place of the moon, and of her apogee, are determined with fo much exactnefs, that it muft have been done by obfervation, either at the inftant referred to, or a few days before or after it. At this time, therefore, it is certain, that aftronomical obfervations were made in India, and that the Brahmans were not, as they are now, without any knowledge of the principles on which their rules were founded. When that knowledge was loft, will not perhaps be eafily afcertained*; but there are, I think,

no

---

* It appears to have been loft, only fince the conqueft of their country by ftrangers; from the want of

Z 4 protection

no circumſtances in the tables from which we can certainly infer the exiſtence of it at a later period than what has juſt been mentioned; for though there are more modern epochs to be found in them, they are ſuch as may have been derived from the moſt ancient of all, by help of the mean motions in the tables of Kriſhna-pouram, without any other ſkill than is required to an ordinary calculation. Of theſe epochs, beſide what have been occaſionally mentioned in the courſe of our remarks, there is one involved in the tables of Narſapour as late as the year 1656, and another as early as the year 78 of our æra, which marks the death of Salivaganam, one of their princes, in whoſe reign a reform is ſaid to have taken place in the methods of their aſtronomy. There is no reference

---

protection and encouragement, and the effects of perſecution and violence. The date ſeems to prove this.

to

to any intermediate date from that time to the beginning of the Kaly-Youg.

" The parts of this aftronomy, therefore, are not all of the fame antiquity; nor can we judge, merely from the epoch to which the tables refer, of the age to which they were originally adapted. We have feen that the tables of Krifhnapouram, though they profefs to be no older than the year 1491 of our æra, are in reality more ancient than the tables of Tirvalore, which are dated from the Kaly-Youg, or at leaft have undergone fewer alterations. This we concluded from the flow motion given to the moon in the former of thefe tables, which agreed, with fuch wonderful precifion, with the fecular equation applied to that planet by Mayer, and explained by M. de la Place.

" But it appears that neither the tables of Tirvalore or Krifhnapouram, nor any
with

with which we are yet acquainted, are the moft ancient to be found in India. The Brahmans conftantly refer to an aftronomy at Benares, which they emphatically ftyle *the ancient*, and which, they fay, is not now underftood by them, though they believe it to be much more accurate than that by which they now calculate. That it is more accurate, is improbable ; that it may be more ancient, no one who has duly attended to the foregoing facts and reafonings, will think impoffible ; and every one, I believe, will acknowledge, that no greater fervice could be rendered to the learned world, than to refcue this precious fragment from obfcurity. If that is ever to be expected, it is when the zeal for knowledge has formed a literary fociety among our countrymen at Bengal *, and

while

---

* I am forry to find, that, fo laudable an example has not yet been followed by our countrymen at

Madras ;

while that society is directed by the learning and abilities of Sir William Jones.—
Indeed, the further discoveries that may
be made with respect to this science, do
not interest merely the astronomer and ma-
thematician, but every one who delights
to mark the progress of mankind, or is
curious to look back on the ancient inhabitants of the globe. It is through the
medium of astronomy alone, that a few
rays from those distant objects can be conveyed in safety to the eye of a modern
observer, so as to afford him a light, which,
though it be scanty, is pure and unbroken,
and free from the false colourings of vanity
and superstition.

Madras; for though Mr. Playfair has emphatically,
and perhaps properly, called the sites of Benares, and
Palibothra, &c. *the classic ground of India*, yet, as the
Southern provinces have been less disturbed by foreigners, than the northern countries of Hindostan,
were due enquiry to be made, I doubt not but many
curious materials would be found in them.

" 3dly,

" 3dly, The bafis of the four fyftems of aftronomical tables we have examined, is evidently the fame.

" Though thefe tables are fcattered over an extenfive country, they feem to have been all originally adapted to the fame meridian, or to meridians at no great diftance, which traverfe what we may call the claffical ground of India, marked by the ruins of Canoge *, Palibothra, and Benares. *They contain rules that have originated between the tropics;* whatever be their epoch, they are all, by their mean motions, connected with that of the Kaly-Youg; and they have befides one uniform character, which it is perhaps not eafy to defcribe. Great ingenuity has been exerted to fimplify their rules, yet in no inftance, almoft, are they reduced to the utmoft fimplicity : and when it happens that the operations to which

---

* Canoge and Palibothra are the fame.

they

they lead are extremely obvious, thefe are often involved in an artificial obfcurity. A Brahman frequently multiplies by a greater number than is neceffary, where he feems to gain nothing but the trouble of dividing by one that is greater in the fame proportion; and he calculates the æra of Salivaganam, with the formality of as many diftinct operations, as if he were going to determine the moon's motion fince the beginning of the Kaly-Youg. The fame fpirit of exclufion, the fame fear of communicating his knowledge, feems to direct the *calculus* which pervades the religion of the Brahman; and in neither of them is he willing to receive or impart inftruction. With all thefe circumftances of refemblance, the methods of this aftronomy are as much diverfified as we can fuppofe the fame fyftem to be, by paffing through the hands of a fucceffion of ingenious men, fertile in refources, and acquainted with the variety and extent of the fcience which they cul-tivated.

tivated.——A fyftem of knowledge which is thus affimilated to the genius of the people, that is diffufed fo widely among them, and diverfified fo much, has a right to be regarded, either as a native, or a very ancient inhabitant of the country where it is found.

" 4thly, The conftruction of thefe tables implies a great knowledge of geometry, arithmetic, and even of the *theoretical part* of aftronomy, &c.

" But what, without doubt, is to be accounted the greateft refinement, is the hypothefis employed in calculating the equations of the centre for the fun, moon, and planets; that, viz. of a circular orbit having a double eccentricity, or having its centre in the middle between the earth and the point about which the angular motion is uniform. If to this we add the great extent of geometrical knowledge requifite to combine this, and the other principles

of

of their aftronomy together, and to deduce from them the juft conclufions, the poffeffion of a calculus equivalent to trigonometry; and laftly, their approximation to the quadrature of the circle; we fhall be aftonifhed at the magnitude of that body of fcience, which muft have enlightened the inhabitants of India in fome remote age, and which, whatever it may have communicated to the weftern nations, appears to have received nothing from them."

If, therefore, after what has been faid, we are obliged to allow that the Hindoos were fo far advanced in the fcience of aftronomy, as to make the obfervations, which they appear to have made, even at the beginning of the Kaly-Youg, about four thoufand eight hundred and ninety years ago; or, according to what has been alledged by M. Bailly and Mr. Playfair, 2400, or 1200 years before that period;

riod; we muſt neceſſarily ſuppoſe many previous ages, in which they might gradually proceed to that degree of knowledge and refinement, which they muſt have then enjoyed. The country ſeems to have been as populous, the nation as powerful, the people as much poliſhed, and arts and learning as far advanced at the *beginning of the Kaly-Youg*, as 4000 years afterwards. But theſe reflections lead us ſo far back into the abyſs of time, that whilſt we are loſt in contemplating the paſt duration of our ſyſtem, we may be apt to forget the generally received opinions with reſpect to the creation of the world, and the hiſtory of mankind.

I ſhall conclude this imperfect ſketch of the aſtronomy of the Brahmans, with an extract of a letter from Sir Robert Barker, to the Preſident of the Royal Society of London, read before the Society the 29th

of

of May 1777, giving a defcription of the obfervatory at Benares *.

'However much that ancient and cele-brated feminary may have declined from its former fplendour, he informs us, that there are ftill many public foundations and tem-ples, where fome thoufands of Brahmans yet conftantly refide.

" Having frequently heard that the Brah-
" mans had a knowledge of aftronomy,
" and being confirmed in this by their
" information of an approaching eclipfe,
" both of the fun and moon, I made in-
" quiry, when at that place in the year
" 1772, amongft the principal Brahmans, to
" endeavour to get fome information rela-
" tive to the manner in which they were
" acquainted with approaching eclipfes ;
" but they gave me but little fatisfaction.

----

* See page 94.

Vol. I.　　　　　A a　　　　　" I was

" I was told, that thofe matters were con-
" fined to a few, who were in poffeffion of
" certain books and records, fome contain-
" ing the myfteries of their religion, and
" others aftronomical tables, written in the
" Sanfkrit language, which fcarcely any
" but thofe few underftand ; that they
" would, however, take me to a place
" which had been conftructed for the pur-
" pofe of making obfervations, and from
" whence they fuppofed the learned Brah-
" mans made theirs. I was conducted to
" an ancient building of ftone, the lower
" part of which, in its prefent ftate, ferved
" as a ftable for horfes, and a receptacle
" for lumber, but, by the number of courts
" and apartments, it appeared that it muft
" once have been an edifice for the ufe
" of fome public body, We entered this
" building, and went up a ftair which led
" to a large terrace on the top of a part of
" it near to the river Ganges, where, to
" my furprife and fatisfaction, I faw a
" number

" number of inſtruments yet remaining in
" the greateſt preſervation, ſtupendouſly
" large, immovable from the ſpot, and con-
" ſtructed of ſtone, ſome of them being
" upwards of twenty feet in height. The
" execution in the conſtruction of theſe
" inſtruments exhibited a mathematical ex-
" actneſs in the fixing, bearing, and fitting,
" of the ſeveral parts. The ſituation of
" the two large quadrants of the inſtru-
" ments marked A*, whoſe radius is nine
" feet two inches, by being at right angles
" with a gnomon at 25 degrees elevation,
" are thrown into ſuch an oblique ſitua-
" tion, as to render them the moſt difficult,
" not only to conſtruct of ſuch a magni-
" tude, but to ſecure in their poſition,
" and affords a ſtrong proof of the ability
" of the architect ; for by the ſhadow of
" the gnomon thrown on the quadrants,
" they do not ſeem to have in the leaſt al-

* See the Plate.

A a 2   " tered

" tered from their original pofition; and
" fo true is the line of the gnomon, that,
" by applying the eye to a fmall iron ring
" of an inch diameter at one end, the fight
" is carried through three others of the
" fame dimenfion to the extremity at the
" other end, thirty-eight feet eight inches
" diftant from it, without any obftruc-
" tion.

" Lieutenant Colonel Archibald Camp-
" bell, at that time chief engineer in the
" Eaft India Company's fervice at Bengal,
" a gentleman whofe abilities do honour to
" his profeffion, made a perfpective draw-
" ing of the whole of the apparatus that
" could be brought within his eye at one
" view; but I lament that he could not re-
" prefent fome very large quadrants, whofe
" radii were about twenty feet, they being
" on the fide from whence he took his
" drawing.   They are exact quarters of
" circles of different radii, the largeft of

13   " which

" which I judged to be twenty feet, con-
" structed very exactly on the sides of
" stone walls built perpendicular, and situ-
" ated, I suppose, in t' meridian of the
" place; a brafs pin i fixed at the centre,
" or angle, of the quadrant, from whence,
" a Brahman informed me, they stretched a
" wire to the circumference when an ob-
" servation was to be made; from which
" it occurred to me, the obferver muft
" have moved his eye up or down the cir-
" cumference by means of a ladder, or
" fome fuch contrivance, to raife and lower
" himfelf until he had difcovered the alti-
" tude of the heavenly bodies in their paf-
" fage over the meridian, fo expreffed on
" the arcs of thofe quadrants; thefe arcs
" are very exactly divided into nine large
" fections, each of them is again divided
" into ten, making ninety leffer divifions,
" or degrees, and thefe into twenty, ex-
" preffing three minutes each, of about
" two tenths of an inch afunder; fo it is

A a 3   " poffible

" poſſible they had ſome method of again
" dividing theſe into more minute parts at
" the time of obſervation.

" My time would only permit me to
" take down the particular dimenſions of
" the moſt capital inſtrument, or the
" greater equinoctial ſun-dial, repreſented by
" figure A, (ſee the Plate,) which appears to
" be an inſtrument to expreſs ſolar time
" by the ſhadow of a gnomon upon two
" quadrants, one ſituated to the eaſt, and
" the other to the weſt of it; and indeed
" the chief part of their inſtruments at this
" place appear to be conſtructed for the
" ſame purpoſe, except the quadrants and
" an inſtrument in braſs, that will be de-
" ſcribed hereafter.

" Figure B is another inſtrument for de-
" termining the exact hour of the day, by
" the ſhadow of a gnomon, which ſtands
" perpendicular to, and in the centre of,
" a flat

" a flat circular ſtone, ſupported in an
" oblique ſituation by means of four up-
" right ſtones and a croſs-piece; ſo that
" the ſhadow of the gnomon, which is a
" perpendicular iron rod, is thrown upon
" the diviſions of the circle deſcribed on
" the face of the flat circular ſtone.

" Figure C is a braſs circle, about two
" feet diameter, moving vertically upon
" two pivots between two ſtone pillars,
" having an index, or hand, turning round
" horizontally on the centre of this circle,
" which is divided into three hundred and
" ſixty parts; but there are no counter-
" diviſions on the index to ſubdivide thoſe
" on the circle. The inſtrument appears
" to be made for taking the angle of a
" ſtar at ſetting or riſing, or for taking the
" azimuth or amplitude of the ſun at ſet-
" ting or riſing.

" The uſe of the inſtrument, figure D,
" I was at a loſs to account for. It conſiſts
" of

" of two circular walls, the outer of which
" is about forty feet diameter and eight
" high, the wall within about half that
" height, and appears intended as a place
" to ftand on to obferve the divifions on
" the upper circle of the outer wall, rather
" than for any other purpofe; and yet
" both circles are divided into three hun-
" dred and fixty degrees, each degree being
" fubdivided into twenty leffer divifions,
" the fame as the quadrants. There is a
" door-way to pafs into the inner circle,
" and a pillar in the centre of that, of the
" fame height with the lower circle, and
" having a hole in it which feems to be a
" focket for an iron rod to be placed per-
" pendicular. The divifions on thefe circles,
" as well as on all the other inftruments,
" will bear a nice examination with a pair
" of compaffes.

" Figure E is a fmall equinoctial fun-
" dial, conftructed on the fame principle as
" the large one A."

Mr.

Mr. Call, member of the Royal Society, and formerly chief engineer on the coaſt of Coromandel, in a letter to the Aſtronomer Royal, to be found in the Philoſophical Tranſactions of 1772, ſays, that he diſcovered the ſigns of the zodiac on the cieling of a choultery at Verdapetah, in the province of Madura, near Cape Comorin; that he found them on the cieling of a temple that ſtands in the middle of a tank, before the pagoda of Teppicolum; and that he had often met with ſeveral parts of the zodiac in detached pieces.

END OF THE FIRST VOLUME.